BLOOD MOUNTAIN

LEO KESSLER

BLOOD
MOUNTAIN

Macdonald & Co
London & Sydney

01470830

A Macdonald Book

First published by Futura Publications in 1978

This Macdonald edition published 1983

Copyright © Futura Publications Ltd 1978

This book is sold subject to the condition that it shall not, by
way of trade or otherwise, be lent, re-sold, hired out or otherwise circulated without the publisher's prior consent in any
form of binding or cover other than that in which it is published
and without a similar condition including this condition being
imposed on the subsequent purchaser.

ISBN 0 356 09488 X

Printed in Great Britain by
Redwood Burn Limited, Trowbridge, Wiltshire
Bound at the Dorstel Press

Macdonald & Co (Publishers) Ltd
Maxwell House
74 Worship Street
London EC2A 2EN

18347920

ACCRINGTON

HYNDBURN

ASSAULT ON A DEADLY MOUNTAIN

'A symbol!'

'What did you say, mein Führer?'

'You heard me, my dear Jodl. Soon our armies will march again; and this time we must kill the Russian monster for good. But my brave soldiers need a symbol, one that the Reds, and those corrupt, cowardly Anglo-Saxons – indeed the whole world – will understand. Something that will symbolize the un-beatable prowess of German arms, and demonstrate that the holy creed of National Socialism cannot be stopped. It must be something . . . something that will transcend all time, will be remembered when you and I are long gone, General Jodl.'

'You speak as if you intend to conquer nature itself, mein Führer.'

'Excellent, Jodl, excellent! What a grandiose idea – the con-quest of nature itself . . . Like the ascent of some hitherto un-climbed mountain. What a symbol that would make for the universe! Nature submitting to the heroic creed of the Na-tional Socialist Movement. The echoes of such a deed will reach the remotest village in the furthest corner of the earth. It would be a tremendous triumph for German arms and our un-beatable movement . . .

JODL, GIVE ME A MOUNTAIN TO CONQUER!

Adolf Hitler to Colonel-General Jodl, his Chief-of-Staff, Spring, 1942.

Section One

A CLIMB IS PROPOSED

ONE

The little Yak observation plane made its third circuit.

Sitting next to the pilot, the officer in the earth-coloured, loose blouse of the Soviet Alpine Corps saw below, a thick wood of tall trees, with scores of well camouflaged tents carefully dispersed among them. Beyond the wood there was the steppe, still winter-bleached and criss-crossed with tank tracks. And on the white ribbons of dusty roads, there were scenes of intense activity. There were field-grey columns everywhere, heading for the mountains, with long slow convoys of tanks and trucks lumbering up behind them.

The young officer bit his bottom lip in dismay.

The pilot, a cocky black-haired, swarthy-skinned Georgian, caught the look. 'Yes, comrade, the sons-of-whores are advancing again. And you don't need to be old Leather-Face to know where they're heading for.'

The Alpine Corps officer ignored the disrespectful description of Marshal Stalin as 'old Leather-Face', though he told himself it wouldn't be long before the NKVD had the pilot in their cellars if he kept on talking like he did.

'Yes, I know, Comrade Lieutenant. They're after the Caucasus and our oil,' he said.

The pilot nodded his head sagely and concentrated on finishing their third circle before levelling out. 'Now what?' he asked, casually ignoring the lazy white tracers which started to curve their way towards them, gathering speed at every moment. 'Do I make another run over the Fritzes?'

The observer, his mind still full of the new German threat to his Motherland, grunted, 'No, Comrade. Now we fly to the mountain.'

The pilot shrugged. '*Horoscho*, comrade. But be prepared to get out and begin walking on air, if this old crate's wings fall off at that height.'

The observer didn't even deign to answer.

The observer pressed his handsome tanned young face closer to the window and gazed down. Now the little Yak was flying over high, rugged country, the naked rock a deep brown against the patches of snow. Here and there, rough country tracks were visible, scratched into rocky hillsides at impossible angles, but roads were few and far between, as he already knew from his study of the maps before he had set out on this reconnaissance mission. He strained his neck and caught a glimpse of a long column of labouring camels, plodding up a steep track.

The pilot grinned, amused. 'Something out of the Middle Ages,' he commented. 'You wouldn't think we were in the middle of a total war, would you?'

'No,' the observer answered, his keen eyes searching a cluster of stone and wooden buildings below, for any sign of life. There was none – the village was abandoned, and he could guess why. The only vegetation up here in the mountains was an occasional patch of withered scrub or gorse, bent at a forty-five degree angle by the tearing wind. The only people who lived in the mountains were the damned Karatski – and everybody knew that they were bandits.

The interior of the little plane started to grow lighter. They were out of the overcast and above the snow-line. From below and above there was the glare of sun and snow. The pilot flipped his sunglasses over his eyes and the smile vanished from his face, as he concentrated on gaining height.

It was a brilliant spring day now. All around the snow-capped peaks shone in the hard yellow sun with a blinding clarity. The observer felt his heart leap. In the good old days before the German invasion it had always been his dream to come here and climb. He knew that the Caucasus Mountains weren't always like this: calm, clear, brilliant. Sometimes the rocks would be as slimy as seaweed with dripping mist, with the wind shrieking like ten thousand banshees, trying with invisible hands to throw the climber off the mountainside. The mountains were like a glorious battlefield, he realized that, illumined by scenes of human treachery, but also of human heroism.

'Comrade, there she is!' the pilot cut into the observer's

reverie, the muscles standing out on his dark hairy arms, as he fought the Yak ever upwards, its radial engine protesting at the effort.

'*Elbrus*!' the observer said reverently and gazed in awe at the great mountain's twin peaks, pink and white against the brilliant hard blue sky.

'Look like a couple of tiny tits, don't they?' the pilot gasped irreverently. 'We Georgians like our women bigger than that.'

The observer ignored the pilot's comment. Little did he know that the highest mountain in the Caucasus range had been called the Elbrus – the Breast – by some long-vanished people because it resembled the female bosom. Instead the observer hurriedly took out his binoculars and started to sweep the range from west to east. But the great field of glittering snow was empty. He adjusted the focus and directed his gaze at the west peak, the higher of the two. Metre by metre, he searched its surface, looking for the signs that they had been there, while next to him the pilot, suddenly grim-faced and sweating, tried to hold the Yak steady in the thin mountain air.

Nothing! Not a sign of them. Ignoring the Yak's sudden upwards surge, the moment of suspension, followed by an abrupt sickening drop, the observer turned his attention to the east peak. Again he searched its surface, hardly hearing the spluttering protests of the overtaxed engine and the pilot's thick curses in his native Georgian. The east peak, at five and a half thousand metres a hundred metres lower than the other, revealed nothing. They hadn't been there, either.

Satisfied, he slipped his binoculars back into the well-worn leather case. His mission was completed. 'All right,' he said expansively, 'take her over now, Comrade Pilot.'

The pilot, his thick black eyebrows gleaming now with beads of sweat, shot him a murderous look. 'Holy Mother of Kazan,' he cried above the spluttering roar of the radial engine, 'have you had your hundred, man?[1] This wooden son-of-a-bitch couldn't cross those tits up there! Her wings would fold up like matchwood.'

[1] The Russian phrase for drunkenness, based on the fact that alcohol is sold in gram units.

The observer from the Alpine Corps shrugged easily. 'You're the mechanic, comrade,' he said, deliberately omitting the 'pilot'. 'Take her back any way you want.'

The sweating pilot did not need a second invitation. While the observer sat back more comfortably in his leather seat, he swung the Yak round in a tight circle and grunted through gritted teeth, 'All right, back over the Fritz lines and down the valley of the River Kuban. And let's hope the field-greys are not waiting for us, this time.'

'They won't be,' the observer answered, with all the supreme confidence of youth. 'In an hour, we'll be home and you'll undoubtedly be filling your guts with fire.'[1]

But the young observer was wrong. There would be no more fiery *Gorilka* vodka for the pilot, and no more mountains for him to climb.

The Georgian was down to a thousand metres, flying through the canyon of the Kuban, when it happened. Behind him lay range after range of snow-covered mountains, as desolate as the surface of the moon. Before him lay the first twinkling pink lights of the front. Once he had crossed them he would be safe. Suddenly a sinister black object hissed at a tremendous speed across his front. He had just time to catch its black-and-white cross insignia, and his heart sank.

'Ass-shit!' he cursed. '*A Fritz fighter!*'

A moment later, even before he had thought of what evasive action he might take in the narrow valley, the Messerschmitt came roaring in, its engine howling. Its machine-guns chattered crazily. Slugs thumped into the Yak's wooden fuselage. The observer screamed, his face a sudden mass of red gore, as he slammed against the side of the cockpit. Desperately the Georgian tried to swing the plane to the side. But the Messerschmitt pilot beat him to it. A burst of fire shattered his tail. He had been badly hit! The Georgian wrestled frantically with the controls. No good! The tail had gone. As the plane started to plummet to the rocky floor of the canyon, the German's final burst of machine-gun fire struck the cockpit can-

[1] Alcohol.

opy squarely. It shattered into a crazy spider's web. Screaming with fear, blinded, blood pouring from his face, the pilot let go of the controls.

With a great rending, tearing crash, the little Yak struck the valley wall, the sound echoing and re-echoing down the length of the chasm, as if it might go on for ever and ever . . .

TWO

'In three devils' name,' Major Greul barked, his breath fogging in the cold mountain air, 'do you men call yourself mountaineers?' He looked down at the troopers in the peaked caps and baggy uniforms of the élite Stormtroop Edelweiss, as they toiled up the sheer rock face, hands on his hips, his muscular legs thrown astride, a look of utter contempt on his hard arrogant face. 'From here you look like nothing so much as a bunch of Munich beer-bellies doing a little rock-scrambling – and badly at that. Now, move it!'

Sergeant-major Meier, known to his comrades, on account of his huge bulk and supposedly thick head, as 'Ox-Jo', whispered to his running-mate, Jap, 'I'd like to move that arrogant bastard – with a push of my alpenstock up his skinny ass!' Aloud, he said: 'You heard the major, you bunch of juicy ballsacks! Get the lead out of your butts and get up that wall!'

Major Greul, Edelweiss's second-in-command, sighed at the big Bavarian NCO's choice of words, but he knew Meier achieved results, and so he turned to concentrate on working out the last phase of their climb to the wrecked Yak reconnaissance plane, somewhere out of sight about three or four hundred metres above his present position on the rock ledge. The forward Luftwaffe base, to which the Messerschmitt pilot belonged, who had shot the Yak down, had immediately notified the 1st Alpine Corps of the 'kill' and had requested its help in searching the wrecked plane for maps and any other information that Intelligence might find useful. General Dietl had naturally turned the assignment over to his élite Edelweiss and he, Greul, had been forced to break off an important training mission to carry out the task.

Most of the pitches had been routine, calling for no more than the usual techniques of the practised rock climber – the knee jam, the press-and-push, the friction hold. All the same, progress had been slow, with constant hold-ups, due to the fact that he didn't know the climb and could only move by a process of trial and error. And time was running out. In an hour it would be dark. He sniffed angrily and stared up at the almost sheer rock face above him. To his right, he could see good holds and what looked like a promising chimney beyond. If he could reach that, he'd probably be able to reach the unseen plane in about thirty minutes.

He made up his mind, just as Sergeant-major Meier reached the ledge below him.

'Meier, are you prepared to try a pendulum?' he asked.

Meier looked down at Jap's wrinkled, oriental face. 'That piece of ape-turd must think I'm a shitting monkey,' he whispered. To the major, however, he called, 'Yessir. Ready when you are.' He braced his feet apart and tightened his hold on the rope which linked him to the major.

Greul, who had climbed his first eight-thousand metre height as a sixteen-year-old Hitler Youth and had conquered the North Face of the Eiger by the time he was twenty, did not hesitate. He reached up, well balanced on both feet, and hammered a piton home into the solitary crack above his head. Letting fall the hammer looped around his wrist, he tried his full weight on the steel hook. It held.

With a practised expert swiftness, he ran a loop of the climbing rope, which attached him to the bull-like NCO below, through a snap ring and fastened the loop to his waist. He was ready to go. Taking one last look at Meier tensed on his ledge, he drew himself back as far and as high as the loop would allow and then he was gone, out into space.

The swing of the pendulum was short and swift. But it sufficed. At the first attempt at the daring manoeuvre he had seized the handhold he had noted to his right. Barely breathing hard, he found a ledge for his feet, and untied the loop. A

14

few minutes later he and Meier had found the entrance to the chimney and had disappeared from sight, while down below, Colonel Stuermer, the C.O. of Stormtroop Edelweiss, lowered his binoculars and cursed softly under his breath. That damned Greul had gotten away with yet another spectacular, and forbidden manoeuvre!

The chimney was tough, but it was no strain. At its opening, it was wide. Palms and back against one rocky side and mountain boots dug into the other, the two Stormtroop men moved up together. Towards its top, however, the chimney narrowed considerably. Greul now took the lead. With his knees dug into the one wall and his broad muscular back against the other, he levered himself upwards, his breathing harsh and loud now with the strain. Once he slipped, and his boots slammed into Meier's guts. Ox-Jo had yelped with the sudden pain, but he had not let go of his own hold. In a flash, Greul, his lean hard face flushed with either shame or effort, had regained his hold, mumbled an apology and was on his way upwards again. And then they were out and sprawled in the snow, shoulder muscles afire with pain, breath coming in great, rasping gasps.

But not for long. Major Gottfried Greul had been punishing and hardening his body with an almost religious intensity ever since he had first heard the harsh Nordic call of the National Socialist creed; he was not a man to allow himself the soft decadent luxury of self-commiseration and rest. Action was his constant slogan. Controlling his harsh breathing by an effort of will, he rose to his feet and commanded: 'All right, Meier. On your feet! Let's get to that plane.'

With a groan, Ox-Jo rose to his feet and began to trail after the major through the deep snow, his broad face brick-red and covered with a film of sweat.

'Look,' Greul exclaimed, as they swung round a slab of grey rock sticking out of the field of immaculate white. 'There it is.'

Meier took in the long broad track, showing where the little observation plane had skidded across the snow before it had come to its final rest. The track was littered with bits of wreckage – a wheel, a chunk of wing with the red star of the Soviet Air Force, a limp shape which he knew instinctively was a body. 'Wonder what the Ivans were farting around here for, sir?' he asked. 'They're bugging out everywhere.'

Major Greul frowned at Meier's choice of words. 'I wish, Sergeant-major, you would learn to moderate your language,' he snapped prissily. 'A National Socialist does not lower himself to use such filth.'

'At your command!' Ox-Jo said mechanically, and mentally told the arrogant major to kiss his National Socialist arse.

'Right, Sergeant-major, you scout around to see what you can find. I'll examine the plane.'

'Yessir,' Meier answered and started to plod through the deep snow, circling the wreck, while Major Greul examined the Yak itself.

The Yak was broken-backed from the impact and it was with difficulty that Greul managed to force open the buckled door of the cockpit. A Russian, the pilot he guessed from the leather jacket the dead man wore, was slumped over the shattered controls, his face a gory mess. Greul grunted. Taking the dead man by his long black hair, he pulled him out of the way and began examining the pockets under the controls for maps.

There were two, but they were both the usual fliers' charts, and both were unmarked. Greul frowned. Where was the route chart and what had the Yak's mission been?

The first question was answered for him a moment later when the Sergeant-major bellowed: 'Sir, I've found the route map.'

Greul straightened up and looked at the big NCO, crying, 'Excellent, Meier, you have done—' The words froze on his lips when he saw what Meier was holding in his other hand.

It was a severed head, complete with Russian Army cap – and the cap bore the insignia of the Red Army's Alpine Corps!

THREE

Colonel Stuermer sat on the ration box in his tent, waiting, and listening to the lazy evening buzz of the camp around him. The big officer in his mid-thirties, who had been one of Germany's leading climbers before the war, always savoured this moment of peace. It reminded him of all the countless times on some ascent or other when he had really been able to let himself go, smoke his pipe, drink his coffee or eat some awful mess of strawberry jam and condensed milk, and forget the awesome responsibilities of leadership.

Stuermer loved the mountains. He loved the physical effort, the danger, the skill and craft one needed, the wealth of memories and the friendships that they created. He liked the responsibility they had thrust upon him, too: the responsibility for a group of brave men, who had to be commanded, not by orders but by example, real leadership and firmness.

But most of all, the mountains meant dignity and freedom for him, removed from the loud, jackbooted, cheap vulgarity of the National Socialist 1,000 Year Reich: clean, wholesome, eternally wrapped in the silence of the deep snow. The mountains, or so it seemed to him as he sat there, quietly puffing his pipe and listening to the sounds of the camp settling down for another night of war, were the last refuge from the evil tide of arrogant aggression, which in these last three years had engulfed the whole of Europe. They were the final escape.

'Sir!'

Stuermer shook himself out of his reverie. Greul was standing at the open flap of the tent. He must have just come back from Corps HQ after completing his mission. 'Come in, Greul,' he snapped, a sudden look of anger on his thin face. 'I want to talk to you.'

Greul entered and replaced the flap carefully. It would soon be dark and the major took the Corps blackout regulations seriously, although the enemy air force had not attempted to bomb them yet, and this was 1942, the second year of the campaign against the Soviet Union.

'Sit down,' Stuermer indicated the other ration box, 'I've something to discuss with you.'

'About this afternoon, sir?' Greul said eagerly, as if he could not contain his excitement.

'Exactly.' Stuermer pointed the end of his pipe towards his second-in-command angrily, as if it were an offensive weapon. 'What in the name of the great whore of Buxtehude were you trying to do this afternoon on that face?'

The excitement vanished from Greul's haughty arrogant face. 'You mean the pendulum, sir?'

'I damnwell do, Greul! You know I've forbidden that kind of trick in this unit.'

'But Meier—'

'Even alpine eagles could get vertigo up there. What if that big ox of a Bavarian rogue, Meier, had got dizzy or lost his balance, Greul? Where would you – and probably he, too – have been then? I'll tell you,' he snapped, answering his own question. 'You would have been a nasty mess on the valley floor, that's where you would have been!'

'Sir, with all due respect,' Greul sneered, 'one can't make an omelette without breaking eggs. In this world one has to take risks to achieve success. Hasn't the Führer himself said many times that only a nation which thinks heroically can win through?'

It was on the tip of Stuermer's tongue to tell Greul what he thought of his damned Führer and such foolishness. But he knew that loyal as Greul was, he was first and foremost a National Socialist. He would not hesitate to report his commanding officer to the Gestapo. Therefore, he snapped instead, 'The Führer is not a mountaineer, Greul. We are, and in *my* unit at least, unnecessary risks will not be taken.' He looked at Greul's flushed face with his hard eyes and said, 'Do you understand that, once and for all?'

Mutely Greul nodded his head, his grey eyes fixed on his dusty mountaineering boots.

For a few moments, Colonel Stuermer let him stew in his

juice, while he listened to Ox-Jo telling one of his disreputable stories to his laughing cronies in what the big NCO probably imagined was a subtle whisper. Finally he broke the heavy silence in the tent. 'Light the lantern, Greul, would you please?' he asked in his normal, polite voice. 'I want to talk to you a little about tomorrow's programme.'

Obediently Greul did as he was commanded, avoiding his C.O.'s eyes as he did so.

Stuermer pretended not to notice. Instead, he spread the little chart in front of him on his knees, saying, 'I don't think I am revealing any great military secret or showing any special insight, Greul, when I tell you that it is certain that the army is going to go over to the offensive pretty soon.'

Greul, a little more at ease now, nodded his agreement.

'And it is obvious where we're heading – for the Caucasus and the Ivans' oil.'

Again Greul nodded his agreement. Outside Meier was saying: *'Then I put my hand up her skirt and you know what I found?'*

'Now the question for us is what role will the High Alpine Corps play in the coming offensive?'

'That she'd got two of them?' a voice queried amid a burst of raucous laughter. Stuermer recognized it as that of Jap, Meier's half-breed running mate. Stuermer smiled and Greul frowned severely. 'Prig', Stuermer told himself and went on to answer his own question.

'So far I haven't been taken into General Dietl's confidence, but one does not need to be a clairvoyant with a crystal ball to guess what it will be. The Alpine Corps will probably be given the job of securing the left flank – the one based on the mountains – of our advance, and Stormtroop Edelweiss undoubtedly will be assigned the mountains to check that the nasty Ivans don't attempt any flank attack with their own alpine troops. Now tomorrow I want the men to practise an emergency climb—'

'But sir,' Greul interrupted, unable to contain his excitement any longer, 'there will be no need for an exercise tomorrow.'

Stuermer looked keenly at the major. 'What do you mean, Greul?'

'We are both summoned to meet with the Corps Commander tomorrow morning at eight hundred hours, sir. General Dietl told me to tell you – and also to have Stormtroop Edelweiss on a two-hour stand-by.'

'Action?'

Greul's grey eyes flashed with excitement. 'It looks like it, sir.'

'But, Greul,' Colonel Stuermer objected, 'the army is not ready to move yet. The units are not all in position by any means, and the necessary supplies are not available in sufficient quantities. My guess is that we will not be able to launch our attack into the Caucasus for another couple of weeks yet.'

'I agree, sir. I think it is something else – perhaps something connected with what we found in that wrecked Russian plane this afternoon.'

'What do you mean?'

Swiftly and eagerly Greul explained how he and Meier had found the dead Russians and how one of them had been wearing the uniform of the Soviet Alpine Corps. Colonel Stuermer sat silent for a few moments in thought after Greul had finished, obviously absorbing the information the major had just given him.

Then he said, 'So you feel that the dead Russian officer was engaged on some sort of recce of the mountains?'

'Yessir.'

'But to what purpose?'

'To launch some sort of flank attack, is my belief,' Greul answered swiftly, 'and my guess is that General Dietl is going to ask us tomorrow, sir, to get up into the mountains and stop them.'

Colonel Stuermer shook his head. 'Impossible, Greul,' he snapped. 'The Russians are on the run everywhere. They are in no position to attack in strength, as you well know. No, an attack is out of the question.' He pointed the stem of his pipe at the major. 'My guess is that probably the dead Russian was trying to find a stop-line – one of the high passes up there in the mountains – where they could stop any attack on our part over that terrain. Yes, that will probably be it, Greul. Tomorrow morning General Dietl will most likely ask us to find and occupy that stop-line before the Russians do. Yes, that will be it.'

Major Greul still seemed doubtful; and in the event both officers would be proved wrong on the morrow. Yet, when Greul had gone, Colonel Stuermer, sitting alone in the tent, sucking moodily at his cold pipe, felt none of the Major's elation at the prospect of fresh action. Instead, he experienced that old sinking feeling of apprehension at the knowledge that he must soon lead good men to their deaths ...

FOUR

'*Meine Herren, der Kaukasus*!' the craggy-faced, skinny Commander of the High Alpine Corps rasped in his thick Bavarian accent, and slapped the map in front of him with his scarred mountaineer's hand. 'At present our troops are stretched across a somewhat loose front between the River Kuban – here in the north – and the Black Sea – in the south – poised, as you can see, at the entrance to the Caucasus.'

Both Colonel Stuermer and Major Greul nodded their understanding, but said nothing. General Dietl had a notoriously bad temper; he didn't take kindly to interruptions during a briefing. Instead they sat on the hard wooden chairs in the small room which had once been some Russian peasant's kitchen and listened.

'It is an open secret that the Führer's summer offensive will head into the Caucasus to seize those vital oil fields. Without more oil the *Wehrmacht* is going to grind to a halt this winter – the Rumanian fields are not enough. Now, as I am sure you have anticipated, the Corps' mission will be to guard the army's flank, to prevent any Russian counter-thrust over the mountains and ensure that nothing will bar the army's progress from that quarter.'

Greul flashed Stuermer a knowing look.

Dietl raised a long finger in warning. 'However, gentlemen, that is not going to be the task of Stormtroop Edelweiss. The Führer has better plans for your unit, Colonel Stuermer.' His craggy face broke into a sudden smile, and Stuermer could guess why. Direct attention from Adolf Hitler could only mean that the Führer was following the progress of the Alpine Corps personally and in its turn that could mean possible promotion for *Herr General der Gebirgstruppen* Dietl. He sniffed, a little contemptuously, and waited for the General's revelations.

Dietl took his time, obviously savouring whatever knowledge he possessed to the full. 'In the last two years our Corps has been given some strange assignments in remote places from Norway to Greece, as you both know. We have climbed and fought in mountains far removed from the rest of the Army. But I think I have never been given a stranger assignment than this. In the middle of a total war to assign men to tackle a peacetime climb, and one that most Westerners would give their eye-teeth to attempt!'

Now Dietl knew he had his two subordinates' attention. Both of them were numbered among the handful of German climbers who had belonged before the war to the international montaineering élite, ranking with the top Austrians and the British. 'As you both know,' he continued, keeping Greul and Stuermer on tenterhooks, 'Soviet Russia was a closed book to Western climbers before the war. Since the Revolution, no Westerner has ever obtained permission to climb here. The Ivans were always afraid that a Western climber might turn out to be a spy in disguise – they have this almost pathological thing about spies.'

Greul clicked his tongue in impatience, eager to be let into the secret. Dietl ignored the sound, enjoying this moment of suspense. 'Now,' he continued, 'the Ivans are no longer in a position to enforce that ruling. We Germans make the rules this year.'

'Yes indeed, sir,' Greul interrupted eagerly. 'But—'

Dietl frowned. 'I shall explain in due course, Major,' he said severely. 'Be patient.' He tapped the chart again. 'Here is

Cherkassy, the foremost position of our troops at the moment. Not more than two days' – perhaps three at the most – march from that town, along the valley of the River Kuban, there is the Elbrus.'

Now it was Colonel Stuermer's turn to interrupt. 'The *Elbrus*!' he echoed, puzzled. 'What possible military value has that mountain for Germany, General?'

Dietl smiled at him bleakly. 'None whatsoever, my dear Colonel,' he answered. 'It would be impossible for the Russians to maintain any kind of military post up there. The peak is well above the snow line and there are easier passes they could use much lower down if they wished to slip troops through the mountains to attack our flank. No, Mount Elbrus has no military value at all.'

'So?' Stuermer asked, a little angry and very puzzled.

'So, Colonel, my Corps – and in particular, Stormtroop Edelweiss – has been given the honour by our Führer Adolf Hitler of climbing Mount Elbrus. As far as I can find out you will be the first Westerners to do so in this century.'

'But why?' both Greul and Stuermer asked in unison, astonished at his announcement that in the middle of a life-and-death struggle between the East and West, they were being asked to go off on a climbing jaunt.

'Because wars are not always won simply by military means,' Dietl answered. 'The war in Russia has dragged on too long. We have lost too many good men here, and much equipment. This year, we must finally break the Russian bear's back or be broken ourselves. But even though the Russians are still retreating, they have a superiority in numbers which we cannot match. We must, therefore, convince them and their many subject peoples that Germany and its soldiers are unbeatable. The Führer wants a symbol – a symbol of German invincibility, which will have such a tremendous moral effect upon them that they will know, whatever their officers and political commissars tell them to the contrary, that there is no hope for them. With luck, when our new offensive in the Caucasus starts, they will break, and come flocking to our colours in their thousands – their hundreds of thousands – as they did in 1941 when we broke through and drove for Moscow.' His voice rose with excitement. ' "Give me the conquest of Mount Elbrus, gentlemen, and I will guarantee you the conquest of the Caucasus" – those were the Führer's own words to me yesterday on the telephone.' The Corps Commander's eyes blazed fanatically. 'Elbrus, the key to the conquest of Southern Russia. A bold blow carried out by a handful of brave men, which will give our Fatherland all the oil it will ever need and might even mean the end of this war this very year. Don't you think that is a gamble worth taking?'

'Of course, General,' Greul responded to Dietl's enthusiasm readily, his own flinty grey eyes gleaming wildly. 'We Germans will show the world that we are unbeatable; that neither man nor nature can stop us!'

Colonel Stuermer's face remained cold. He did not share the other two men's vulgar dream – the conquest of a peak as a symbol of national superiority. For him it was yet another example of National Socialist Germany's contemptuous élitist thinking. Icily, he said, 'Naturally Stormtroop Edelweiss will carry out any mission assigned to it, sir. But aren't you forgetting one thing, General?'

'And what is that, my dear Stuermer?' General Dietl asked in high good humour.

'The fact that yesterday a member of the Soviet Alpine Corps reconnoitred Mount Elbrus. What are we to make of that?'

General Dietl's look of self-satisfaction vanished abruptly, but he remained silent. He had no answer ready to that particular question.

FIVE

'*Piss pansy!*' Sergeant-major Meier bellowed, as the truck hit yet another hole in the terrible road that led into Cherkassy. 'Can't yer watch what yer doing? My kidneys are floating in my throat already.'

Jap wrestled with the wheel of the ancient Opel truck and narrowly avoided a deep rut in the unsurfaced road. 'Shut up, you Bavarian slime-shitter,' he said through gritted teeth. 'Can't yer see I'm doing the best I can? It's not my shitting fault that the shitting Popovs build such shitting lousy roads.'

'Yer'll get a knuckle sandwich planted in the middle of your ugly yeller kisser if you talk like that to me, ape-turd. Don't yer know you're in the presence of a senior NCO of the High Alpine Corps.'

'Up yours!' was the sweating little half-breed corporal's sole reply, as he spun the wheel round to avoid another bump.

Meier gave a mock sigh, looked morosely out of the window, and said, 'No respect these days in the German Army for old long-serving NCOs, who have given their all for Fatherland, Folk and Führer. No respect at all.'

'What do you think this lark's all about, Ox-Jo,' Jap asked, as the outskirts of the town began to come into sight ahead of them – a collection of shabby, white-painted cottages with straw roofs, surrounded by tumbledown picket fences, the gardens almost hidden by the tall yellow sunflowers.

'Search me, Jap,' Meier answered, idly glancing at the houses, most of which seemed abandoned. 'The C.O. told me to get down here and round up what mules I could find – that's all. The rest of the troop would follow in twenty-four hours. Now what do you make of that?'

Jap changed down before answering, 'Well, of course, you Bavarians are known to have bird-brains, so I'll put it to you nice and simple. If we're to look for mules, that means that wherever we're going, it wouldn't be by truck, right?'

'Right,' Meier agreed, eyeing with interest the first woman he saw: a barefoot, dark-haired beauty, with a heavy bosom for such a youngster. 'She's got plenty of wood in front of her door,' he remarked appreciatively. 'I'd like to get my head between them and go *brr*!'

'Perverted Bavarian barn-shitter – she can't be a day over twelve!'

'As old as that?' Meier said, as the girl disappeared from view. 'Watch yer tongue, you Chinese crap-can, or yer'll be lacking a set of ears before we get where we're going.'

'As I was saying,' Jap continued, unmoved by the threat, 'if we're walking, where are we walking to!'

'You tell me, smartass,' Meier said and launched a juicy, noisy kiss at a heavy-set woman bent over a wash-tub and revealing sturdy, muscular legs with plenty of white thigh above. 'Get a load of those pins, Jap. I bet they go right up to her ass!'

'So, if we're walking and we need mules for transport to carry our gear,' Jap went on purposefully, changing down to second as they entered Cherkassy's main square, 'you can guess where we're heading for?'

'Natch,' Meier said casually, as the dust-covered Opel rolled to a stop in front of the *Kommandatura*.[1] 'Up there!' He pointed a forefinger like a sausage at the white gleaming peaks of the far mountains. 'Now come on, let's see what these base stallions can do about finding us our four-legged friends.'

The two of them, Ox-Jo and Jap, sat in the dusty square, drinking *Airan*, sour mare's milk, which Ox-Jo had described aptly as smelling like a 'mixture of cow shit and pig sweat,' watching the barefoot boys and girls drag in the reluctant mules to the big, red-faced police NCO, who handed them a bundle of worthless Occupation roubles for the animals.

'Look at 'em, Jap,' Ox-Jo said lazily, bored with Cherkassy, bored with the drink, bored with the war, pointing at the little brown mules. 'Did you ever see a worse bunch of knock-kneed, knackered—'

He stopped suddenly. A woman had entered the square, as tall and majestic as a high priestess, leading a fine brown mule, advancing through the crowd of scruffy, barefoot boys and girls, as if they weren't there. Meier took a quick gulp of the sour mare's milk, as if his throat were suddenly parched, and gasped. 'Get a load of the lungs on that one! *Wow*, she's just my collar-size!'

'And what about me?' Jap protested.

But Meier was already on his big feet, sweeping the civilians

[1] Town HQ.

aside to left and right as he descended upon the unsuspecting Russian woman. Taking off his peaked cap, with the silver badge of the *Edelweiss* on its side, and sweeping it in front of him in a low bow, he said happily: 'My name is Meier. I am a senior NCO of the Greater German *Wehrmacht,* and I love you. Shall we go to bed now?'

Unlike the local women, this one was blonde and blue-eyed, with a fine chiselled nose. For a moment her handsome, determined face showed rage and disdain at the boldness of this importuning giant of a German, then for some reason she glanced at his cap, and her look changed to one of agreeable pleasantness. 'You are very gallant, Sergeant-major,' she said in excellent German.

Meier's big face flushed a deep red, and behind him Jap chuckled, 'She's gone and caught yer with yer skivvies down, Ox-Jo, eh?'

Meier, normally no respecter of persons, was definitely embarrassed now. 'Excuse me, I didn't know . . . I thought you wouldn't understand . . .'

The big blonde woman smiled. 'Soldiers will be soldiers, Sergeant-major. German as well as Russian, they want only two things of a woman – and the second one is food.' And with that she swept by the crimson-faced NCO, leaving him standing there open-mouthed.

'What's the matter with you, you asparagus Tarzan?' Jap asked, as the two of them sat on the stoop of the little cottage in which the *Kommandatura* had billeted them.

It was now evening, and the blood-red ball of the sun was beginning to slip down behind the mountains, tinting the snow-covered peaks with dramatic pink. The few civilians still about were hurrying back to their shabby homes before the curfew came into force. Any civilian found on the streets after nine o'clock was shot automatically, without trial. The *Wehrmacht* was too frightened of the Soviet partisans, reputed to be in the area, to take any chances.

'It's that Popov woman,' Ox-Jo answered, dragging slowly

at his cigarette. 'I think I've fallen in love. At least my eggs are giving me jip.'

'And what about me?' Angrily Jap spat out his cigarette butt. 'I haven't had a bit for so long that I'm beginning to think those mules aren't so bad-looking after all.'

'Ah, but the difference between me and you is that I'm a senior NCO – and besides, you are half a foreigner, anyway,' he added, alluding to Jap's Sherpa father whose brief liaison with a Bavarian farm girl had resulted in the wrinkled, yellow-faced corporal, 'and that sort of stuff is too good for a foreigner. Only us Germans qualify for that kind of lovely grub.'

Jap sniffed. 'At any rate, you'll have to keep it tied to yer right leg, this night. You don't know where she lives, or whether she'd spread her pearly gates for you, even if you did. Besides, if the chain-dogs catch you after dark, they'll have yer behind Swedish curtains before yer feet can hit the ground.' He spread his dirty yellow fingers in front of his face to symbolize the prison bars.

'A couple of ruptured, crappy old military policemen don't frighten Mrs Meier's son when he's in love,' Meier said contemptuously. 'But I've got to know where she lives.'

'What's it worth to you?'

'What do you mean – what's it worth to me?' Meier demanded, looking round at him curiously.

'Well, I think I could help you, for a small – er – consideration.'

Meier held up a fist like a small pink ham. 'Now, none of that, Jap. I know what you mean by a small consideration. You're not getting any of that. I've told you already I love her – and you simply don't share the woman you love, even with your best pal.'

Jap's face fell. 'Well, then, that's that, I suppose,' he said.

'Now come on, Jap,' Meier wheedled, 'you wouldn't let a mate down like that? How do I find her?'

'Is it worth three jumps to you the next time we get to some place where they have a *Wehrmacht* knocking-shop?'

'Three jumps, Jap – that's a lot of moss! Fifty marks at least.'

28

Jap shrugged eloquently. 'Take it or leave it. Imagine what it'll be like for me, while you're there dipping your wick in all that honey! All that I'll have to keep me happy is five against one and the old five-fingered widow is getting a bit boring, I can tell you that.'

Meier gave in. 'All right. When you're in love, you're prepared to sacrifice anything for your beloved.' He beamed at the little half-breed. 'I read that in a book once,' he announced proudly.

'You shouldn't have bothered,' Jap said sourly. 'For three jumps at the knocking shop, I'll tell you. You see the *Kommandantura*,' he began to explain, as if he were talking to a very small and very stupid child. 'You go in there and down the corridor. To the right, you'll find a little office, and in the little office, you'll find a fat chain-dog with a red hooter, which he'll explain to you is red because he's got a bad cold, but which is in fact the result of too much indulgence in strong waters—'

'Oh, get on with it,' Meier interrupted impatiently. 'My eggs are really acting up with all that love juice.'

'Well, you say to the chap with the red hooter, discreetly passing him over a pack of twenty cancer-sticks as you do so, that you are looking for a long-lost maiden aunt, whom you will describe as being tall, blonde and having a well-endowed balcony—'

'Of *course*!' Meier blurted out exuberantly. 'All these Popovs have to be registered with the local German bulls! That chain-dog will know where everybody in a little dump like this is located. Now why didn't I think of that?'

'Because you're as thick as two oaken planks, that's why. Now don't forget—'

But Sergeant-major Meier was no longer listening; he was already running in the direction of the *Kommandantura*.

The woman was not surprised in the least when he came blundering through the door of her little cottage, without knocking, a packet of stolen Army sausage under one arm and a double litre bottle of black market vodka under the other, crying as he did so, 'Food and drink – *and me* – for my beloved!'

Lazily she slid her legs from under her on the ricketty sofa, revealing a delicious glimpse of creamy white inner thigh and black silken panties as she did so. 'I've been expecting you,' she said in a thick throaty seductive purr. 'Take your clothes off.'

With one hand she released the single catch that held up her skirt. With the other she clicked off the light. In the sudden darkness, Sergeant-major Meier sighed in awe, as if he had just been informed he was to be admitted to Paradise.

SIX

'Well, Haas?' Colonel Stuermer snapped. 'But please stand at ease.'

Lieutenant Haas, the Stormtroop's newest officer, shot out the right foot of his immaculately polished mountain boots and flashed his C.O. a quick smile of thanks. 'Well, sir,' he said, waving his hand at the piles of equipment stored in the shed, 'I've been through the lot three times. Boots, crampons, ice-axes – everything – and I am pretty sure we've got everything.'

'Only pretty sure?' Stuermer asked quietly. He liked the boy, whose father had been a celebrated Alpine Troop commander in Italy in the First World War; he didn't want to play the typical heavy C.O. with him. Haas flushed.

'You see, Haas, in an operation like this, complicated by the fact that we are also at war, one single oversight can spell disaster.' He bent down to the pile of ropes and rummaged through them for a few moments, while the young officer watched him nervously. Finally he straightened up, a smile on his face. 'I was just checking if you had included a Prusik sling. You know, if one of those big-footed mountain boys of mine fell into a crevasse we'd need the Prusik to get him out. I see you've got one. Good.'

Lieutenant Haas looked at his C.O.'s lean, sunburnt face

with its sensitive chiselled mouth and the blue eyes which could be so cold, yet so compassionate, and was glad – in spite of his ever-present fear – that he was going into action for the first time under the command of such a man. 'Thank you, sir. I really did make a careful inspection.'

'Of course, you did. Now come along, Haas, let us break the happy news to the men.'

Happily the young officer followed his C.O. outside. The weather was brilliant and hot; all the same, the snow still gleamed on the far peaks. It would take more than this heat to melt the snow up there, Stuermer told himself, and returned the waiting Meier's tremendous salute with a casual gesture. 'I see you've got sentries posted, Sergeant-major,' he said.

'The Ivans have got big ears, sir,' Ox-Jo replied. 'Thought it better they didn't hear anything which would give them ear-ache.'

'Good idea, Meier.'

'I'm not just a pretty face, sir,' Meier answered with a smirk. He tapped his temple. 'There's a brain up here as well.'

'Some people will believe anything, I suppose, Meier,' Stuermer said in high good humour and opened the door to the big barn in which he would give his briefing. With a crash of heavy, nailed boots on the wooden floor, which sent up a cloud of ancient dust, the men of Stormtroop Edelweiss stamped to attention.

Greul swung his commander an immaculate salute and bellowed at the top of his voice, as if he were back on some Prussian parade ground. 'Stormtroop Edelweiss, two officers, sixteen NCOs and sixty men. All present and correct, *sir*!

'Thank you, Greul,' Stuermer answered coldly, wishing that Greul would not attempt to play the new kind of brutal, aggressive National Socialist officer. He looked at the men's faces. They were hard, bronzed and tough: the faces of the world's best mountain troops, every one of them born and bred in the Bavarian Alps, where male children absorb mountain lore and skill with their mother's milk. 'Morning, soldiers!' he said with forced cheerfulness, feeling again the awesome re-

31

sponsibility of attempting to ensure that these men returned one day to their mountain homes.

'Morning, Colonel!' they sang back in hearty unison.

'Please sit down.' Stuermer nodded to Greul, and as the soldiers squatted on the wooden floor, the major whipped away the blanket which covered the map attached to the wall.

Stuermer let his men have a good look at the big map before he commenced his briefing. 'Comrades, we have been given a mission by the Corps Commander himself.' He tapped the map. 'Here Mount Elbrus is located – all five thousand, six hundred metres of it. We have been given the task of climbing it, not for any military purpose, but as a symbol of German superiority and heroism!'

While the barn buzzed with excited chatter, Stuermer could not help but look at Greul. But his irony had had no effect. The major's face glowed with vulgar pride. Stuermer raised his hands to stop the chatter. 'Now you must not think we're off on some peacetime climbing jaunt.' Again he tapped the map. 'Before we even reach the foot of the mountain we will have to pass through some fifty kilometres of enemy territory. As far as we know, the Red Army has evacuated the area in its retreat into the Caucasus. But there are still the partisans to reckon with, and, according to Intelligence, the Karatski tribe located around the hamlet of Chursuk – here!' He tapped the map. 'By tradition they are bandits, and Moslems to boot. Therefore they were against the Reds, but that doesn't mean automatically that they will be for us. And, again according to Intelligence, they have some pretty unpleasant habits with their prisoners.'

'Oh, don't tell me, sir, that I'm going to be a singing tenor if they get their paws on me!' Meier squeaked in a falsetto voice, clutching the front of his baggy grey trousers to make his meaning perfectly clear.

'Yes, something like that, Meier,' Stuermer agreed, joining in the burst of laughter which had greeted the Sergeant-major's remark. 'Though the thought shouldn't worry you. The way you've been going at it these last few years, it's bound to drop off of its own accord anyway, one day!'

His sally brought forth another burst of laughter. But it wasn't shared by two men there: Greul, who was prudish to an extreme, and young Lieutenant Haas, whose face revealed all too plainly his sudden fear.

Stuermer's face grew grave again as he continued. 'Providing we have no trouble at Chursuk or before that, we'll begin the real business of climbing once we are through the Chotyu Pass – here. It's about three thousand metres above sea-level, and in spite of the good weather we've been having of late, we can assume there'll be snow up there still. With a bit of luck, however, we'll be able to reach Elbrus House – here – by the end of the first day.'

'A house, sir?' Jap queried.

'Yes,' Stuermer answered, seeing the puzzled look on the little half-breed's yellow face. 'Apparently the Russians had begun building it at the beginning of the war. Supposed to be covered with aluminium or some sort of alloy to make it proof against the kind of weather you can expect in winter at four thousand odd metres. It was intended as a weather station, but whether the Russians were able to complete it, we don't know.'

'Is it occupied, sir?' Meier asked.

'Again, we don't know that, Meier. At all events we shall rest the second day and prepare for the ascent to the West Peak – here. At five thousand six hundred and thirty-three metres, it is the real summit. The other is a hundred metres lower.'

'Look like a couple of tits,' Meier said. 'We should call it Twin-Tit Mountain. Imagine the headlines in Berlin, sir, once we've climbed it – *Stormtroop Edelweiss Plants Swastika on Right Nipple of Twin-Tit Mountain.*'

'Sergeant-major Meier,' Greul barked above the laughter, his lean face flushed with anger, 'must you mouth such filth – and insult our flag, to boot?'

'Just trying to cheer the chaps up, sir,' Meier replied easily, unmoved by the major's angry outburst.

'Leave the cheering up of the chaps to me, please, Meier,' Stuermer said quickly, and continued. 'I'm not going to risk taking the whole unit up that peak. Once we're in the house I'll pick a good dozen of the fittest of you for the ascent. With luck, we should be able to be up and down in a day, though the ascent will be a matter of trial and error. Intelligence has been unable to turn up any Russian material on the difficulty of the climb and no one in the West has attempted it since the Russian revolution.'

'Has it ever been climbed at all?' Haas asked curiously.

'I don't know. I should imagine that someone might have attempted it – the Russians have some excellent climbers, though we know little about their exploits – their Government never allowed them out of the country for an international climb.' He smiled at the boy. 'We'll give you the honour of carrying the flag up the mountain, Haas. That'll get you in the record books. If I recollect correctly, your father had a dozen eight thousands [1] to his credit.'

'Yessir, he did. And thank you – for the flag,' Haas mumbled, a little red in the face.

His father, Haas thought as the Colonel continued his briefing. How he wished he could be like the giant old colonel, bluff, jovial and without one little bit of fear in his still muscular body! All his life the old colonel had sailed from one adventure to another, shrugging off the danger, supremely confident that nothing could go wrong. His father would never have understood the fears that had plagued *him* ever since the time the old colonel had taken him on his first ascent at the age of five, his stomach knotted and constricted in that nameless terrifying fear that he was to come to know so well in the years to come. He had learned to hide his fears; the old colonel would have never believed that a son of his could ever suffer from a dread that was completely unknown to him. But Lieutenant Haas knew well that one day, somehow and somewhere, he would not be able to conceal his fear – and then that would be the end for him.

'But remember this,' Colonel Stuermer was saying, 'we are at war, though from the mission we have been given I have my doubts that the base stallions at the FHQ [2] really realize it. We

[1] Eight thousand metre climbs.
[2] Führer Headquarters.

34

will keep one eye on the summit of Mount Elbrus, but at the same time, we must also keep an eye to our rear.' He looked around at his men's faces, which were abruptly very serious. 'Just in case some nasty Ivan partisan decides to stick a knife in such a tempting, unguarded target.'

Lieutenant Hass shuddered. But no one, least of all the C.O., noticed: an oversight, which was going to have disastrous consequences for Stormtroop Edelweiss . . .

SEVEN

The next thirty-six hours flew by. There were a hundred and one minor and major problems for Colonel Stuermer to solve – from the ammunition he could expect each man to carry once they had commenced the ascent, to whether they should take salt tablets (against heat exhaustion) or not. For now the summer sun was there in full strength, and in the suddenly oven-hot air of the plain, from which there was no relief, the half-naked mountaineers sweated over their equipment, preparing to load it on the drooping, listless, brown mules.

Colonel Stuermer longed for the cool of the far mountain peaks. But, his lean face already brick-red from the sun, he forced himself out into the burning sunshine to inspect and check the mountaineers' preparations. And from early morning to late evening, the sun continued to blaze down mercilessly, the heat waves trembling on the still air, the mountains in a stifling opaque haze.

It was not surprising that when Major Greul sneered at a sweat-drenched, exhausted Lieutenant Haas, who was acting as the Stormtroop's supply officer, 'My God, Haas pull yourself together in front of the men,' Colonel Stuermer rounded on the surprised Major with, 'Greul, can't you ever remember you are a human being – and that human beings have weaknesses?'

'Weaknesses, sir?' Greul echoed, puzzled.

'Yes, weaknesses. You and your cheap ideology! Do you

35

think that is what war and the mountains are about? The creation of a new master race, who use the possibility of death as a kind of political and national aphrodisiac?' With an angry gesture, Stuermer wiped the sweat from his burning face. 'The mountains prove nothing – they are just there. Remember that!' And with that, Colonel Stuermer strode away to inspect another group of mountaineers grouped around a reluctant mule, leaving Greul staring after him in open-mouthed bewilderment, while a grinning Haas went back to work with renewed energy, confident that his C.O. was the best in the whole of the Greater German Wehrmacht.

At the end of the second day of preparations, Colonel Stuermer called Stormtroop Edelweiss together and told the weary men that the preparations were finished. 'You can take the next twenty-four hours off. We shall move out after dark, as soon as the curfew is enforced tomorrow evening. But one thing: remember the peasants in the village seem to be friendly – so far they have been very co-operative – yet we still can't take any chances. For that reason – everybody is confined to camp for the next twenty-four hours. And I mean *everybody*! Good, dismiss!'

Most of the men were only too glad to lie down in the shade of their bunks, away from the blinding sun and the backbreaking work of the last forty-eight hours. But not all. Sergeant-major Meier, for one, had other plans for that night. As he said to his running-mate Jap, who was stretched out completely naked on his blankets, exhausted, arm shielding his eyes from the last rays of the sinking sun which came in through the hole in the wall that served as the cottage's window, 'I mean, you lot of warm brothers don't like women. I do. Besides it'll be a long time till I get another bit of how's yer father – and I think I love Roswitha,' the big NCO added thoughtfully. 'As soon as it's dark I'm off under the wire.'

'Love her?' Jap said wearily. 'You big currant-crapper, you've only known her a week!'

'In wartime, love blossoms quick,' Meier announced. 'I read that in a book once.'

'*Books!*' Jap snorted. 'It takes you all yer time to read the instructions on a packet of Parisians.' [1]

'Well, by the look of that nasty little worm you've got drooping there, *you'd* never need a Parisian. They don't make 'em for midgets.' He rose from the bunk, and walked across to the tin basin of grey suddy water on the chair in the corner. 'Better start making myself more beautiful for Roswitha. And remember to cover up for me when the orderly officer comes round – tell him I'm in the thunderbox or somewhere – or I'll dock that worm of yours down to the size of a maggot!'

'Hope she's given you a nice juicy case of clap,' replied Jap in his usual friendly manner, 'that'll certainly make love blossom even faster ...'

Roswitha was waiting for him as usual when he slipped into her little blacked-out cottage, lying on the couch, naked save for a pair of black silken knickers, her ivory-white body glowing in the dusky red light given out by the solitary candle under its red glass shade.

'Firewater?' she enquired.

Meier took his greedy eyes off her beautiful naked body and looked for the usual bottle of vodka. It was standing on the top of the green-tiled oven. Grabbing it, he took a hefty slug straight from the bottle. 'Grr!' he breathed gratefully. 'That was good. The dust was up to my tonsils.'

'You have been working hard today, yes?' she asked carefully, still not moving.

'Yes.' He grinned knowingly and advanced upon her, taking off his clothes as he did so. 'But I know I'm going to work a lot harder for the next thirty minutes. Come here, my little Russian cheetah!'

Quivering with what the big NCO took for passion and desire, the Russian woman allowed him to fondle her breasts. She sighed with pleasure at his touch. His hairy paws grabbed for her black knickers and ripped them off in one swift greedy grab. '*Nyet!*' she gasped.

'Don't be impatient – soon,' he gasped, misunderstanding

[1] Slang for contraceptives.

her protest, grappling with his boots as he forced her backwards.

'*Boshe moy – nyet!*' Her fervent protest ended in a hysterical, gurgling scream, deep down in her throat, as he thrust himself savagely between her wide-open legs.

It was nearly dawn now. Outside, the birds were beginning their first frantic chatter of welcome to the new light. Eyes half-closed, weary, and yawning constantly, as if he would never really wake up again, a tousle-haired Meier searched unwillingly for his clothes, while the Russian woman, lying naked on the rumpled sofa, watched him, half-amused, half-wary. 'You have duty this morning?' she asked as he pulled on his boots and began to thread the laces through the brass-rimmed holes.

'No,' he said thickly.

'Why the hurry, then?'

'We're not allowed out of camp. I am here without permission. I must get back before everyone wakes up.'

She nodded her pretty blonde head. 'Is there something happening there?'

Meier was too busy trying to tie his boots to notice the sudden gleam of interest in her eyes. 'I think we're leaving.'

'For the mountains?'

He looked at her suddenly, aware of her persistence. 'How do you know – the mountains?' he asked.

'I don't know,' she answered, shrugging easily. 'Just your badge. The Edelweiss. Everyone knows that alpine flower is the badge of the German alpine troops. So, if you go anywhere – you go to the mountains. Yes or no?'

Meier ignored her question. 'Don't you worry your pretty Popov head about such things,' he said. He clasped her to his uniformed chest. 'Listen. I'll come out with the driver to get bread from the bakehouse up the road for the soldiers at midday. It'll take about half an hour to load up the loaves. Can I come by for a quickie?'

'Quickie?' she queried.

'You know, Roswitha. *Bang-bang, goodbye ma'am.*' The

big Bavarian NCO made an explicit gesture with his thumb pressed between his two forefingers.

'Oh, yes, I see . . . Yes. I will be here for you.' She smiled, but there was no accompanying warmth in her bright blue eyes.

'Fine.' He planted a big, wet, noisy kiss on the side of her cheek. 'Off I go to the big war. See you at mid-day, Roswitha.'

'*Dosvidanya*, soldier,' she sighed wearily and watched him go, never to return, as she had watched many of their proud field-grey backs depart in these last terrible twelve months. Then, snapping out of her momentary reverie, she started hastily to put on her clothes.

Punctually at twelve o'clock, a happy smiling Sergeant-major Meier clicked open the gate to her little cottage and knocked politely on the door. There was no answer. He knocked again – and again. Still no answer. Puzzled, and not a little disappointed, for he knew at the back of his mind he would never see the handsome blonde Russian woman again after to-day, he opened the door and said, 'Roswitha, it's me – and I'm limping already.'

There was no answering call.

'Perhaps she's in the thunderbox,' he said to himself, and opening the door of the kitchen he looked out at the little wooden lean-to with the crude heart carved in its door. It, too, was empty. The girl was nowhere to be found.

In his few bits of fractured Russian, with the aid of much arm-waving and exaggerated gestures, he tried the neighbours on both sides of the tumbledown cottage. They were obviously frightened, and there was nothing he could get out of them about Roswitha's strange disappearance. Over and over again, they kept repeating the same word '*schpion*', '*schpion*', which meant nothing to him until, as he walked disconsolately back to the waiting truck, its meaning dawned upon him. '*Schpion*' was the same as the German Spion.[1]

He paused in the middle of his stride, and staring blankly at the dirty white wall in front of him, he said to no-one in particular, 'Roswitha is a spy!' He bit his bottom lip in bewilder-

[1] German for 'spy'.

39

ment. 'But for whom – and what did she want to know?'

There was no answer forthcoming to those particular questions. Watching the German's strange behaviour from the open door of his bakery, the sweating, flour-covered baker in his dirty undershirt tapped his temple and said to himself: 'The Fritzes – they're always either drunk or crazy – or a bit of both...'

EIGHT

'All right, you bunch of wet-tails,' Meier called, 'get those twinkle-toes of yours moving! Make dust!'

Colonel Stuermer sighed. 'Meier, must you make so much noise? You'll waken half of Southern Russia with that foghorn of yours!'

Meier peered at him through the gloom. 'Sorry, sir. Just doing my duty as a conscientious NCO of the Greater German Army should.'

'I shit upon you, Meier,' Stuermer said, sensing rather than seeing the mocking look on the big Bavarian's face. 'From a great height!'

'Thank you, sir. I appreciate your concern for my well-being.'

'Get on with it, you rogue.' Stuermer chuckled and turned to the elderly one-armed colonel in charge of the *Kommandantura* who stood next to him, framed in the yellow light streaming from the door of his quarters. 'Well, I suppose this is the parting of the ways, Colonel.'

'Wish I were going with you, Stuermer. But with this one flipper of mine, I don't suppose I'd be much use to you where you're going.'

Stuermer knew the elderly Colonel was happy he was staying behind. He preferred his nightly bottle of vodka, his warm bed, and the even warmer young Russian girl who shared it with him. All the same, Stuermer said, 'I wish you could come along with us too, Colonel. We can always use good men. But someone must keep things ticking over in the rear echelon, you know.'

'Spect you're right, Stuermer,' the colonel said, his mind already occupied with the thought of Lydia's naked body, waiting for him under the covers upstairs, once Stormtroop Edelweiss was gone.

Stuermer took one last look at his men lined up in a long column in the blacked-out gloom, with the mules at the rear under the command of Lieutenant Haas, their hooves and equipment wrapped in sacking so that they would make as little noise as possible as they passed through a sleeping Cherkassy. Then he turned back to the colonel. 'Many thanks once again for everything you have done for us while we were here.' He swung his opposite number a salute. 'Till the next time, Colonel.'

'Till the next time, Stuermer – and lots of luck.'

'Thank you.' Stuermer turned and strode away. He gave a soft command to Major Greul, who was in charge of the point.

'Broken step!' Greul ordered. 'Advance!'

Shuffling through the ankle-deep dust, the men and mules started to advance. Like silent ghosts, they disappeared one by one into the darkness.

At the door to his quarters, the old one-armed colonel watched them for a few moments, his mind full of Lydia. Then he turned and closed the door behind him, licking his suddenly dry lips in anticipation. But Colonel August Adams was not fated to enjoy the ample charms of his eighteen-year-old Lydia that night or any other night.

The blonde woman waited till the last plodding mule had shuffled past, its head bowed as if it bore not only its load but all the cares of the world, before she whispered, '*Now!*'

Dark clouds parted in the moon's path for an instant, and she could see the men all around her, tensed over the knives and axes, as they started to creep towards the *Kommandantura*. Metre by metre they crawled towards the silent bunker which was the HQ's sole defence. She clutched her own pistol more firmly in a hand that was beginning to sweat heavily with nervousness, and followed.

They were about fifty metres from the bunker now. There was no sound save the soft whisper of the wind in the tall oaks. Abruptly the blonde woman froze. Two dark shapes had detached themselves from the deep shadows cast by the oaks. Slowly they plodded towards the crouching men, in the slow, weary manner of soldiers everywhere who were carrying out a boring duty in the middle of the night. Carefully, very carefully, she cupped her hands around her mouth and whispered in the ear of the man nearest to her, 'Fritzes, Sergei.'

'I've seen them already,' the boy whispered back. 'Shall I take them out, Comrade Captain?' His stainless steel teeth flashed in a grin.

'Yes.'

Sergei needed no urging. He gripped his knife between his steel teeth and crawled forward, while she watched his progress tensely, knowing that they would have a real fight on their hands if the sentries managed to alert the bunker in time. But her fears were groundless.

Just as the first of the elderly sentries turned, probably alarmed by some slight noise Sergei made, the boy flung himself forward. His knife flashed. There was a stifled cry of pain. The first sentry sank to his knees, clutching his slit throat, trying to stem the sudden flow of blood. Sergei sprang on the other one's back, gripped the rear of his coal-scuttle helmet and tugged hard. It was an old partisan trick. The Fritz's chin strap would dig into his neck and effectively cut off any shout of warning.

The woman waited no longer. 'Forward comrades!' she hissed, while Sergei wrestled the dying German to the ground.

The men swept forward like grey, hungry timber wolves emerging from some winter forest, greedy for prey to still their gnawing hunger. A partisan kicked the kneeling German in the face. He smashed against the nearest tree and was dead before he hit the ground. Behind the first partisan, another one sprang over the dead body and flung open the door to the bunker. A third knew exactly what he had to do. The captured grenade flew from his hand. In the same instant that it hurtled into the inside of the bunker, the man at the door slammed it closed again. There was a thick throaty crump from within.

'Into the *Kommandantura*!' the woman cried above the noise. They hurtled up the steps. A half-naked German came running towards them, trying to pull up his braces over his fat belly as he did so. Sergei's knife flashed once more. He went down, his throat slashed open from jugular to the carotid, drowning in his own blood. Sergei gave the woman another of his gleaming steel smiles of triumph.

'Up the stairs!' she commanded.

Followed by half a dozen of the partisans, she clattered up the staircase. A German opened a door, pistol in hand. Before he could fire, a partisan tommy-gun chattered. He jack-knifed, stomach ripped open by the vicious burst, and flopped over the landing rail.

'This way,' the woman gasped. She knew the way to the one-armed Fritz colonel's room exactly. With the heel of his boot, Sergei smashed in the door.

The one-armed Colonel was completely naked, standing next to the rumpled bed in which cowered a pretty baby-faced girl, who couldn't have been a day older than eighteen.

The woman was suddenly seized by an all-consuming rage. It was pretty obvious what the one-armed Fritz had been about to do when they had burst in, and it was clear, too, that the girl had been a willing party to his disgusting form of fornication. '*Pigs – vile pigs*!' she hissed through clenched teeth and pressed the trigger of her pistol.

The bullet struck the Colonel in the stomach. He smashed back against the wall, eyes wide and staring, pink foam suddenly on his lips, a gaping hole vivid red against the pale white of his stomach. She fired again. This time she did not miss her target.

The Colonel's sexual organs shattered in a red flurry of flesh and blood. He screamed once like a pig being castrated and slammed to the floor.

'*Boshe moy*!' Sergei said in awe, as he stared at the hole in the base of the Colonel's stomach.

The woman turned her burning eyes on the girl cowering in the bed, the felt quilt drawn up in front of her, as if that fragile thing might protect her from what must come.

'Let me have her first, Comrade Captain,' Sergei pleaded. 'I'll give her one good meal of real Russian meat after all that Fritz carrion.'

The woman ignored his plea. She raised her still-smoking pistol. The girl backed against the headrest, as if she might be able to press herself through it and escape. *'Comrade . . . Comrade . . . please Ros—'*

Her frantic request for mercy was cut short by the sharp crack of the pistol. She screamed as the slug shattered her pretty white face like the shell of a soft-boiled egg being struck by a too heavy spoon. Her lifeless body slumped on the quilt.

The woman savoured this moment. It seemed to her at that instant that her action had purified her beautiful body of all the dirt it had accumulated in these last terrible months when she had been no different from the girl she had just murdered. She had killed herself! Then she snapped out of her reverie. 'Collect all their weapons and distribute them to the peasants!' she cried. 'Come on – hurry it up there. There is a lot to be done yet . . .'

And far away at the tail-end of the Stormtroop column, young Lieutenant Haas heard the faint sound of firing to their rear and felt an icy finger of fear trace its way down the length of his spine. Instinctively he knew what had just happened. Behind them the road to the rear had been cut. They were on their own in Russian-held territory. There was no way back.

Section Two

A TRAP IS SPRUNG

ONE

'Sir!'

Colonel Stuermer swung round on Sergeant-major Meier who was marching behind him at the point of the long slow column of mules and mountaineers. 'Yes, Meier? What is it?'

By way of an answer, Ox-Jo pointed a big finger at the foot-hills to the right of the road that led to Chursuk. Outlined a stark black against the crimson ball of the late afternoon sun, a handful of riders were plodding along on a parallel course to their own.

'Must be well over a couple of kilometres away,' Meier confirmed what Stuermer was thinking. 'In this mountain air, you can see much further than in the plains.'

Stuermer nodded, and flinging up his glasses, focussed them on the mysterious riders. There were a dozen of them, mounted on ponies not much bigger than their own mules, and as far as he could make out they wore no uniform. But it was clear that the dark objects they bore across their shoulders were rifles. They were an armed party.

The question was who were they?

It was a question that Major Greul aired a moment later.

'What do you make of them, sir?' he asked, lowering his own binoculars.

Stuermer did the same slowly. 'Don't know exactly, Greul. They could be partisans. They could be this tribe – the Karat-ski – that Intelligence mentioned.'

'One thing is certain though, sir,' Meier interrupted. 'They know we're here – and they're watching us.' He pointed his finger at the sudden bright gleam that came from the ranks of the strange riders. 'Binoculars.'

'Yes,' Stuermer agreed. 'You're right there.' For a moment he stood there, his brow creased in a puzzled frown, while the column came to a halt behind him. Then he made his decision. 'There is nothing we can do about them. We're on foot, they're mounted. Meier?'

'Sir?'

'Pass the word back – everyone is to keep his eyes peeled, and you and Jap better hoof it to the rear of the column to give Lieutenant Haas a bit of muscle – just in case.'

'Right, sir,' Meier said cheerfully, and nudged his running mate. 'Come on, we're going to have a look at mule arses from behind. It'll be better than looking at your ugly mug all the time.' Holding onto their machine pistols, the two NCOs doubled the length of the column, passing on the C.O.'s orders, while the men of Stormtroop Edelweiss checked their weapons in anticipation.

But nothing happened. As that long afternoon passed, the riders kept level with the column, but made no attempt to attack it. After a while the mountaineers gave up their regular glances in their direction and concentrated on the march towards the glittering peaks of the snow-covered mountains, above which the still air seemed to shimmer an electric blue.

As the afternoon started to draw to a close, and the temperature began to become bearable, the character of the country also changed. The steppe became more broken. Grey rock outcrop was more frequent and the grass grew yellow and stunted, as if it had been pressed down for a long time by the winter snows. Here and there a sweating trooper buttoned up his tunic, shivering a little at the cooler wind which was blowing from the mountains, in welcome relief from the almost unbearable heat of the steppe.

Just before nightfall, Stuermer ordered a stop near a pleasantly babbling mountain stream and when the tired troopers stumped sore-footed to it, they found the water icy-cold, as if it had originated in one of the far-off glaciers. As Jap complained through suddenly chattering teeth: 'Cold enough to freeze the eggs off yer!'

'Yes, if yer had any to freeze off,' Meier agreed, pouring a canteen of the icy water over his big head.

Standing a little way from the men grouped around the stream quenching their thirst and bathing their sore tired feet, Stuermer surveyed their position.

The place was as good as any for an overnight camp. The

area was littered with small boulders – probably the result of some Ice Age moraine – with solid tufts of large thistles dotted here and there between the boulders. It would make an ideal defensive site just in case.

For the first time in the last hour or so, he remembered the strange riders who had accompanied the column for most of the afternoon. He swung round and focussed his binoculars on the hills to their right. Screwing up his eyes against the almost horizontal rays of the setting sun, he searched every nook and cranny. Without success. The riders had vanished as abruptly as they had come. A few moments later the sun slipped behind the hills and the valley was swamped in darkness. Stormtroop Edelweiss was alone again.

They had eaten the last of the pea soup, washed their canteens in the stream and now, with the stars glittering a hard silver in the immense purple sweep of the sky above them, the men of Edelweiss lay in their blankets, drifting off to sleep.

Colonel Stuermer lay next to young Haas, his head resting on his rucksack, fully dressed save for his boots, thinking over the events of the day. Far away he could hear the faint howl of the timber wolf. Idly he wondered if it could have any significance. A warning perhaps?

'Do you think we'll reach Chursuk tomorrow, sir?' Haas broke into his thoughts.

'Very probably, Haas. With a bit of luck.'

'But those riders, sir. Do you think they could be partisans?'

Stuermer misunderstood the anxious note in the young officer's voice. 'Don't worry, Haas, you'll get to climb the mountain,' he said with a soft chuckle. 'Remember, I promised you you'd carry the flag on the ascent.'

'Thank you, sir, but . . . but perhaps I won't be good enough for a climb like that.'

Again Colonel Stuermer chuckled. 'Don't worry, any son of Colonel Haas is good enough. Your father would have my hide, if I refused to let his son in on something like the ascent of Mount Elbrus. God forbid!'

Lieutenant Haas remained silent and again Colonel Stuermer misunderstood. 'Your father is of the old generation. Almost nineteenth century,' Colonel Stuermer went on, unaware of the young officer's real reasons. 'The English started climbing, you know. The rich sons of the fat bourgeoisie. They were sick of the commercialism of city life. They wanted a new challenge – a new dimension of existence, the English climber Edward Whymper called it. On the one hand, they wanted to get away from civilization, and on the other, climbing mountains was a sort of symbol that human beings could tame nature, even the highest peaks. Your father belongs to that generation. I understand his motives, but I don't quite agree with them.'

Lieutenant Haas turned in his blankets and stared through the velvet gloom at the white blur of Colonel Stuermer's face. How he wished his father were like the colonel: a man to whom he could talk openly, express his inner fears, his emotions, his weaknesses! 'Why don't you agree, sir?' he asked softly.

'Well, I agree in the sense that it is good to get away from civilization – remote from city squalor, the noise, the purposeless activity of buying and selling. But the conquest of nature. No! Nature is simply there, it is nothing that you can fight and conquer. That is a kind of philosophy to which I cannot subscribe. It smacks—'

'Of the brown uniform and the crooked cross,' the young Lieutenant beat him to it.

'Perhaps,' Colonel Stuermer agreed, and smiled softly. Haas knew; he had seen through him. 'But, my dear Lieutenant, I think we'd better drop that particular subject for this night. After all, one can't have a unit commander talking treason with one of his officers, can one?'

Haas laughed softly and a little nervously. 'No, one can't, Colonel.'

'Good night, then, Haas. Up at five tomorrow.'

'Good night, sir,' Haas replied, feeling reassured and confident again. 'And thank you, sir.'

Colonel Stuermer turned on his side and made himself more comfortable on the hard stony ground, but he didn't close his eyes immediately. 'Thank you sir,' the boy had said. He wondered idly: Why?

Slowly the Stormtroop men fell asleep. Now there was no sound in the little camp save the snores of the weary mountaineers, the soft tread of the sentries and the crackle of the watch fires. Above them in the heights, the watchers counted the number of fires and carefully noted their positions. The woman was a stickler for details; she wouldn't tolerate any carelessness. Thus they watched and waited.

TWO

Sergeant-major Meier raised his right leg and gave a soft fart. '*Heil Hitler*,' he said automatically.

'Shut up!' Colonel Stuermer whispered. 'Do you want them to hear, you stupid lout?' He waved his pistol. 'Follow me.' Together with Ox-Jo, Jap and six of his veterans, he began to steal into the thin night mist which writhed through the boulders, their sock-covered boots almost noiseless. They waded a little torrent, its rushing water again drowning any sound they might have made. On the other side, Colonel Stuermer knelt and ran his hand over the damp earth. His fingers traced the outline of what he had expected to find there – a horse-hoof mark.

'They're up this way,' he whispered to Ox-Jo, 'and remember when the balloon goes up, I don't want corpses, I want prisoners.'

The big NCO clutched the sandfilled sock he had prepared specially for this night's excursion more firmly in his ham-like fist, and whispered back, 'Never fear, sir, you'll get one – handed to you on a silver platter.'

They went on, the track becoming more difficult. Stuermer veered to the right, telling himself that whoever was watching them would need a clear field of sight over the camp below. They worked their way through a group of mountain pines, carefully lifting each branch and holding it until the man behind could catch it and do the same for the man coming after him. The method was almost soundless, in spite of the thickness of the trees.

Stuermer was holding the last pine branch when his nostrils were suddenly assailed by the warm sweet smell of horses. In that same moment, they must have scented him. There was a faint whinny and the sound of a fretting horse pawing the earth. He froze. They were there. The unknown watchers could only be a matter of metres away. He crouched low and slid into the glade. Before him, there was a line of boulders, with beyond, far down below, the faint pink flickering of the mountaineers' campfires. This was the observation site. He began to crawl forward. Behind him his men emerged one by one, and veterans that they were, they split into two groups, intent on converging on the boulders from both sides.

Now Colonel Stuermer's nostrils picked up the scent of unwashed human bodies and the stinking black *Marhokka* tobacco the Russians smoked. They were very close now. He could feel the sweat begin to break out all over his lean body, in spite of the coldness of the night. And he knew why. It was at the prospect of violent action.

The horses, tethered somewhere out of sight beyond the boulders, obviously sensing that the strangers represented danger, continued their fretting and nervous low whinnying. But the unknown watchers seemingly were asleep. There was no reaction from their positions. Colonel Stuermer told himself they must be amateurs. Even partisan units usually put out sentries when they slept. But then perhaps his own trick of leading out this little patrol in the middle of the night, when the rest of the Stormtroop had been asleep for hours, might well have lulled the watchers into a false sense of security. He crept on, body tense and tingling, expecting the shout of alarm and fear to come at any moment.

It did. The very next moment. But from a quarter he had not expected. Suddenly he stumbled and nearly lost his balance. At his feet, a pale blur of face stared up at him in shocked surprise. For what seemed an age, the two men stared at each other, soundlessly, motionlessly. Stuermer recovered first. Just as the Russian opened his mouth to sound the alarm, Stuermer's pistol clubbed down on his head. With a soft moan, he flew back into the hole grubbed in the stony earth in which he had been sleeping.

But the moan was enough. Beyond the boulders, the horses reared up in alarm, tugging and jingling their traces, whinnying with fear.

'*Stoi?*' a voice broke the silence.

Stuermer knew they had been discovered. 'At them!' he cried.

Sleeping men woke up startled. Here and there a man managed to scramble to his feet before the attack descended upon them. A Russian tried to grapple with Ox-Jo. The big NCO didn't give him a chance. His blackjack smashed into the back of the Russian's head. He fell, as if pole-axed. A man broke away from the furious mêlée. Instinctively, Stuermer knew he was heading for the tethered horses. Stuermer jerked the trigger of his pistol. Scarlet flame stabbed the darkness. The running man faltered, his hands fanning the air, spine curved in unbearable agony. Then, as the light vanished, he flopped to the ground, face-first.

Another man broke loose from the scene of murder and mayhem. Stuermer pulled the trigger. No one must escape, he knew that. Nothing happened! Angrily he pressed it again. Once more nothing. He swung round to Jap, who was acting as his bodyguard. '*Fire – damn you!*' he roared. Jap did not hesitate. The machine pistol chattered in his hands. The running man zig-zagged violently, vicious spurts of sparks thrown up at his heels. But the man bore a charmed life. Just as Ox-Jo slugged the last Russian into insensibility, the running man disappeared behind the cover of the far boulders. A moment's silence. Next instant there was the frantic clatter of horse's hooves down the stony trail that led to the valley. Stuermer let his shoulders slump, suddenly feeling very tired. The Russian had got away. He would warn the others, whoever they might be.

'All right, shithouse mouse,' Ox-Jo snarled, drawing back his big fist. 'Sing, or you'll get the biggest knuckle-sandwich you've ever eaten!'

Their sole prisoner, the man Colonel Stuermer had stumbled across, stared back at the big NCO numbly, his face gleaming with sweat in the light of the torch that Jap held. He shook his head.

The Stormtroop corporal, who spoke some Russian, repeated the question that Stuermer had posed. 'Who are you and what is your mission?'

Again the man shook his head.

Before Stuermer could stop him, Ox-Jo dropped his fist. He pulled out his pistol and cracked the muzzle against the prisoner's mouth. With a yelp of sudden pain, he opened it. In a flash, Ox-Jo's pistol muzzle had penetrated into his throat and thrust him back against the rock-face. Gagging and choking, trying to free himself from the gun, the man's head writhed back and forth as Ox-Jo cursed him roundly in his thick Munich accent.

Colonel Stuermer had had enough. He understood Ox-Jo's reason for using this kind of method to extract the information they needed. Time was short. The man who had escaped might already be bringing up reinforcements. This was not the proper place for a long-winded interrogation. All the same, he could not tolerate torture in Stormtroop Edelweiss.

'All right, Sergeant-major,' he snapped, 'that's enough!'

'But sir, I've just got the perverted banana-sucker where I want him,' Meier began to protest.

'I said that's enough!' Stuermer cut him short. 'Let him go, do you hear?'

Meier did as he was ordered. The prisoner sank to his knees, face wild with pain, bloody, pulpy tissue spewing from his wide-open, frantic mouth.

Stuermer licked his lips. 'Ask him the question once more, Corporal,' he commanded in a weak voice. 'If he doesn't talk, we're getting out of here.'

The interpreter repeated the question.

The prisoner looked up at the circle of hard faces, hollowed

54

out to death-heads in the blue light, and probably told himself he could expect no mercy from them. They would kill him if he didn't talk. He spat out a broken tooth, and a gob of thick blood, and began to speak.

Hastily the corporal translated; he, too, wanted to be on the way back to the camp before the escaped Russian returned with his comrades. 'He says, sir, that he belongs to a partisan group . . . They were formed in the winter . . . They have units all over the south . . . they are supplied by air.'

'Ask him why they were watching us?' Stuermer asked. Far away he thought he could hear the clip-clop of horses' hooves picking their way with difficulty, up the steep trail in the darkness.

The Corporal translated swiftly.

Again the prisoner spat out blood. Now his answer came more slowly. Perhaps he, too, had heard the sound of horses. 'I was ordered to, that's all he says, sir,' the corporal interpreted.

The clatter of hooves was getting louder now. 'Who ordered him to watch us?' Stuermer flung a last question at the prisoner. The prisoner seemed about to refuse to answer. Ox-Jo raised the bloody muzzle of his pistol threateningly. The Russian gulped. He spoke.

'Well?' Stuermer demanded, when the interpreter did not speak. 'Who?'

'A woman, sir. A blonde woman from Moscow,' the corporal answered, his face puzzled.

And then as the first wild bullets began to howl from the boulders all around them, the men of Stormtroop Edelweiss were scrambling for safety back into the trees, leaving their one-time prisoner unconscious in the blood-stained dust.

THREE

Major Greul had had the men awake and ready to march off, as agreed with Colonel Stuermer, when he had heard the sound of the small-arms fire above, in the mountains. Together with

55

the sweating, hard-breathing little patrol, they had disappeared into the night, their haste communicated even to the normally slow-moving mules, followed by the wild erratic fire of the new group of partisans. They had escaped without a casualty, and after a while the firing had died away altogether, and they had been able to slacken their pace to the normal sixty paces a minute.

Now it was mid-afternoon, and at the point, Colonel Stuermer, narrowing his eyes against the glare of the sun, could just make out the blue wisps of lazy smoke emerging from the *isbas*.[1] They were arriving at the village of Chursuk. He decided to take no chances. Placing two troops under the command of Major Greul, he ordered him to secure the heights on both sides of the dusty winding country road. Then, assuming command of the rest, and followed at a distance of five hundred metres by Lieutenant Haas and his mules, he began to advance on the village.

The clip-clop of the mules' hooves started the skinny-ribbed dogs, lolling outside the decrepit huts, off barking: the racket wakening the inhabitants of the huts who had been sleeping. Barefoot, shaven-headed boys, with slant dark eyes, came out, scattering the chickens which shared the huts with them, and gawped open-mouthed at the newcomers. Heavy-bosomed women in rags, their dark faces almost hidden, save for the eyes, by cloths hastily flung across them in the Muslim fashion, followed – and a few men. And Colonel Stuermer noted out of the corner of his eye that most of them were armed. Was he leading Stormtroop Edelweiss right into a trap? The thought flashed through his mind alarmingly. 'Keep a weather-eye peeled, Meier,' he snapped at the big NCO who followed at his heels, together with Jap, who because of the Mongol-cast of his features, which he had inherited from his Sherpa father, seemed to be attracting most of the attention.

'Will do, sir,' Meier replied promptly, and unslung his machine pistol significantly.

They passed on into a kind of rough square, with the houses built into the side of the rock wall above them and supported

[1] Primitive cottages.

by rough-hewn, weather-worn timbers. To Colonel Stuermer's mind, it would be an ideal place for an ambush.

He raised his hand and the dusty column halted. He would go no further, especially as his progress was barred by a group of men, dirty, unkempt, with bloodshot drunkard's eyes, who, like the ones he had spotted earlier, were all armed. 'Everybody on his toes,' he commanded. 'But nobody fires unless I give an order to.'

For what seemed an age, the ragged scowling bunch of tribesmen and the tense, anxious mountaineers faced each other in the hot rays of the sun in the dusty square, in complete silence. Suddenly there was the sound of many horses' hooves. It was followed a moment later by the crackle of small-arms fire. 'Stand to' Colonel Stuermer ordered urgently, as the crowd parted, and about fifty horsemen came riding full tilt, firing their ancient pieces above their heads as they did so.

'*Hold it!*' Stuermer yelled above the racket just in time, as the horsemen jerked at their reins and brought their sweat-lathered mounts back on their haunches in a slither of pebbles and a cloud of dust, sliding to a halt. The Karatski were putting on a demonstration of strength for his benefit.

For a few moments more, the wildly excited dirty horsemen continued to expend their ammunition, while their frenzied, wild-eyed horses spun round in crazy circles. Then, one by one, the ancient curved-butted rifles started to fall silent, until no one was firing.

Stuermer heaved a sigh of relief, and stared up at the dirty bearded faces of the sweat-stained horsemen. They were definitely un-Russian in appearance, with their high cheekbones and slant eyes. No one in Intelligence had been able to tell him much about the Karatski, but one didn't need to be clairvoyant to know that they were from the East, perhaps the last survivors of one of the great oriental scourges which had swept across Russia in the old days.

But the big colonel had little time to speculate about the origin of the horsemen. Suddenly one of them swung himself down from a white stallion heavily decorated in antique silver braids, and dropped neatly in front of Stuermer. '*Bandit*,' he announced. '*Ya Starost.*'

'He's the headman here, sir,' the corporal translated. 'His name is – er – Bandit.'

'Well, I'll piss up my sleeve,' Meier whispered to the colonel. 'He shitting well looks like it too, sir!'

Stuermer agreed. The headman certainly did, with his long yellow face, terrible squint and long, drooping, Mexican bandit moustache, obviously dyed, hanging down on both sides of a sly mouth. Hoping that appearances did not always count, he said to the interpreter, 'Tell him, Corporal, that we come as friends. Tell him that although we represent the mighty German Army, we will allow him and his men to keep their weapons, providing they use them only against our enemies – the Russians.'

'Circumcise your watches!' Meier breathed, in awe at the colonel's boldness when the little force of mountaineers was clearly outnumbered by the wild riders. 'You certainly know how to lay it on, sir.'

Stuermer ignored the NCO's comment. His eyes were fixed on the headman's face for his reaction. Although he didn't understand the words, the yellow man's reaction was obvious enough. At the mention of the word '*russki*', he hawked thickly, spat in the dust and drew one dirty forefinger slowly along his throat as if he were slitting it. The headman was definitely no friend of the Russians.

The corporal took a long time interpreting the headman's speech, in which he explained he and his people had always been the enemies of the Russians, presumably as far back as the days of the legendary Rurik. But in the end he finished his diatribe, which was replete with much hawking and spitting, and clapped his hands.

As if by magic, a barefoot, shaven-headed boy appeared, bearing a silver tray, obviously looted somewhere or other on one of the tribe's rampages down into the plains. On it was a crisp loaf of white bread, salt and two glasses of vodka.

Stuermer knew the tradition. In the old days when Germany had first invaded Russia, the advancing troops had been welcomed thus by headmen at the entrance of every village. But when the population had begun to realize that the Greater German Wehrmacht had not come as liberators from the Communists, but as new conquerors, the custom had ceased. He took the loaf, tore a strip off it, and swallowed it. Then, placing a pinch of salt in the 'V' of taut skin formed by stretching his thumb and forefinger round one of the glasses of vodka, he licked the salt, raised the glass in toast to the headman, who had taken the other glass, and downed the firewater in one fast gulp.

The ice was broken. The wild-looking tribesmen applauded by slapping the butts of their weapons against their horses' sweating flanks and the celebration could begin.

Woman after woman entered, bearing tray upon tray of food, mutton, raw and pounded to a kind of stinking paste, boiled, or roast and pungent with garlic. Great mounds of the crisp white bread of the area. Huge casks of honey. Bowls of water, drawn directly from the River Kuban and grey with the tiny pebbles that it contained. Steaming gourds of warm mare's milk – and alcohol, for although the Karatski were supposedly Muslim, and from the window of the barn in which the Stormtroop had been billeted they could see the wooden mosque, they seemed to have no objection to alcohol. On the contrary, the road outside was already littered wtih 'vodka corpses' and the tribesmen constantly kept falling out of the saddles of their mounts, overcome by too much vodka.

But if their men were wild and unhibited, the women were modest, silent and invariably veiled with a piece of cloth covering their faces between the mouth and the eyes. Yet there was no concealing their interest in Jap. Their black eyes flashed with interest, every time they passed the place where he squatted on the floor, and he received the largest portions of food and drink. Once or twice the women overcame their shyness sufficiently to touch his yellow face, as if they were reassuring themselves that his colour was real. In particular, Jap received the attention of the *Starost*'s daughter, a tall, wonderfully built young woman, of whom Meier said: 'I'd give her a piece of my salami any day – for free, too!' She could hardly keep her eyes and hands off the little corporal, who munched away at his food on the floor in greasy-lipped contentment. In the end she leaned across and whispered something in the interpreter's ear, and incidentally gave an appreciative Jap a generous look at her melon-sized breasts, before fleeing in embarrassed confusion, giggling as she ran out.

'What did she say?' Jap asked, his mouth full of roast mutton, the grease dribbling down his unshaven chin.

'She said, she liked you most. She said you were one of them.'

'Yer,' Ox-Jo snarled, showing his envy. 'I always knew he was one of *them*.'

'Yellow is mellow,' Jap said, unmoved, and accepted another leg of steaming roast mutton from one of the admiring females. 'Yellow is very definitely mellow up here.'

'What do you make of them, sir?' Lieutenant Haas asked Colonel Stuermer, as the latter and Greul sipped the warm mare's milk reflectively.

'Well, I don't think friend Bandit is exactly Andre Hofer,' [1] Colonel Stuermer answered. 'I mean they are out-and-out robbers. They do no work. That, they leave to their womenfolk. Their occupation is hunting and robbing. But because of that, they seem to have come into conflict with the powers-that-be ever since the days of the Czar. And I think for that reason they have been traditionally anti-Russian and now anti-Soviet. He took another sip of his *airan*. 'As far as I could make out from the *Starost*, the Red Army launched a punitive expedition against his people – there are a couple of hundred thousand of them altogether – just before the war. They managed to beat the Reds off, but they suffered severe casualties. That expedition seemingly has made them more anti-Russian than ever. At all events, that Bandit chap appears to want us here.' He waved a hand at the red-faced, gorged mountaineers.

'*Appears!*' Greul emphasized the word with a sneer. 'To

[1] An Austrian Tyrolean national hero, who fought against Napoleon in his native mountains.

my way of thinking they are just as sub-human as the rest of the Red rabble. I don't think you can trust a single one of them.'

'You might be right, my dear Major,' Colonel Stuermer said. 'But for the time being we must not show them that we *distrust* them. What is it that that American said? *"Walk softly and carry a big stick"*? This whole expedition puzzles me. First that business in the mountains last night. Who is the woman? And remember that Soviet Alpine Corps cap you found in the plane. What of that? And now these people. They look like villains, yet they welcome us as if we are long-lost cousins.' He finished the last of his drink, and yawned. 'We will play the role of the happy, welcomed visitor, but we will be on our guard as long as we are here in Chursuk. We will carry a big stick.'

'Wooden eye, be on thy guard,' Haas said, pulling down the side of his right eye in the German gesture of caution. 'Is that it, sir?'

'Exactly, Haas,' Colonel Stuermer said, rising to his feet. Everywhere the drunken soldiers attempted to rise, but he waved them to remain seated. 'Carry on, soldiers,' he commanded and looking down at Greul's face, set in its usual look of contempt for such drunken indulgence, he said, before leaving for his bed, 'Ensure that Sergeant-major Meier runs a security patrol this night, Greul. I want no more unpleasant surprises to disturb my nocturnal slumbers.'

Greul looked at Haas's grinning face. 'Does something amuse you, Haas?' he snapped.

'Not really, sir.'

'*Not really,*' Greul echoed harshly. 'A German officer and a National Socialist is never vague. It is either one thing or the other for him. Well?'

Haas flushed. 'I was just thinking, sir,' he stuttered, 'that the C.O. does everything with a . . . a certain sort of style. I mean, he never takes things beer-seriously.'

'Meaning I do?'

'No, I didn't say that, sir.'

'Well, now I'm going to be *beer-serious*, as you put it in that common soldiers' slang you prefer to use. Lieutenant Haas, you will take charge of this night's security arrangements.' He rose stiffly to his feet, eager to be away from the scene of drunken carousing.

Haas sprang to attention. 'Sir!'

Greul gave him one last look. 'Remember, Haas, you are in charge. Now I bid you good-night.' And with that, he strode out in his usual imperious manner, leaving Haas staring after him, suddenly very afraid.

FOUR

'*Kr..unt*!'

Jap staggered up to his feet drunkenly. All around him, his comrades lay snoring where they had fallen, in a heavy drunken sleep. He shook his head. The bone-littered room came into focus, looming at him out of the drunken fog. He shook his head again and wished he hadn't. His head started to throb rhythmically, like an overworked outboard motor. Slowly, very slowly, he creaked his head round, as if it worked by heavy weights.

The 'vodka corpses' lay sprawled everywhere, hands still clutching their glasses, draped like broken puppets across upturned trestle tables, slumped, like over-grown grey embryos, in corners. There was even one trooper lying lengthwise across the pot-bellied iron stove at the back of the room, the steam rising slowly from his vodka-soaked uniform, giving off the unpleasant stink of smouldering serge. 'Suppose the stupid shit must be cold,' Jap told himself, drunkenly.

Then the picture of those two melon-sized breasts flashed in front of his eyes, and he remembered why he had woken up. The *Starost*'s daughter! He gave a low growl. '*Kr..unt*,' he cried hoarsely. '*Must have . . . kr..unt this night!*'

One yellow paw stretched out in front of him, unaware that he was clad only in his boots and tunic, he staggered towards the door like a blind man feeling his way, crunching across the bones which littered the floor, stumbling over the unprotesting bodies of his comrades, his mind full of those magnificent breasts, which seemed to fill the whole world, like two huge yellow zeppelins.

He flung open the door and blinked. It was pitch-black outside. He blinked again and, undaunted, stepped out into the night, realizing, as the cold mountain air struck his hot face, that he was more drunk than he thought. Still, he staggered on through the narrow silent streets, already playing with those great breasts, balancing them in his hands, as if he were judging the weight and sweetness of sugar melons, juggling them up and down like a circus clown, sticking them in each ear and crying *'I've gone deaf – I can't hear a thing!'*

The row of cliff-like houses in the little village square came into view, outlined a starker black against the jagged silhouette of the mountains beyond. He stood there, puzzled, swaying back and forth, a cold wind breezing about his naked rump, trying to puzzle out which was the *Starost's* house. His eye fell on the yellow candle flickering in one of the little windows. For a moment he could not believe it; then he gasped, 'She knew I was coming . . . She lit a candle for me!'

He blundered forward eagerly, his mind already stripping the *Starost's* daughter, with the exotic beauty lying in her bed, completely naked, her legs slightly parted, her lips red and wet with passionate anticipation. *'Never fear, my beloved,'* he called to no-one in particular, *'Your Jap is coming.'* He laughed uproariously, *'But not yet. You get the joke?'* The words froze on his lips. He had bumped into a solid rock wall. For a moment or two he searched it, mumbling to himself, 'Who's taken the shitty house away . . . Come on, put that place back again, eh?'

Then it dawned on him, after minutes of fumbling along the rock wall, that the houses were built above the stone. 'Of course,' he reassured himself drunkenly. 'She wouldn't try to cheat me . . . She loves me.'

He stood, considering the problem. She was waiting for him up there, her naked nubile body tormented with passion. But how was he to reach her? Suddenly he remembered. The tribesmen reached their houses by a rope ladder that they could draw up in time of trouble. Groggily he searched around until he found the knotted rope, which hung just above his head. He reached up and grabbed it, but found that the strength seemed to have gone from his arms. For what seemed a long time he just hung there, the wind whistling around his naked rear, puffing, sweating and swearing like an angry yellow-faced monkey.

'I'm coming up, if it shittingly well kills me,' he cursed, the sweat dropping into his eyes like vinegar, his shoulders feeling as if they were going to be dragged out of their sockets at any moment.

He summoned up the last of his strength, heaved, and pulled himself onto the ledge above, to lie there gasping and sobbing, while one of the fat pigeons which the Karatski kept, stared at him, cooing softly, wondering whether this little yellow man who had turned up from nowhere in the middle of the night was dangerous.

'Make dust, you feathered fart!' Jap snarled, and flapped one hand weakly at the bird.

It flew away, squawking.

Jap staggered to his feet, and nearly fell over the side, catching himself just in time. He looked to his right. There was the yellow light, all right. His first instinct was to rush straight in and snuggle right up to her. Then he remembered what the colonel had said about the unpleasant treatment the tribesmen sometimes handed out. He shuddered. It would be like jumping too low over a too-high fence. He couldn't chance that. Tip-toeing forward with the exaggerated caution of the drunk, he approached the flickering light.

As he crept closer, he became aware of the low murmur of several voices. '*Not that*!' he exclaimed, stopping in his tracks, as if he had just stood on a sharp nail. '*She hasn't betrayed me? No!*'

For what seemed a long time, he couldn't bring himself to move any further; he knew he couldn't bear the knowledge that she was in the sack with another man. He ran his mind over the possibilities, anger now beginning to fire his blood. Not that big Bavarian bastard Meier! He'd be the only one in Edelweiss who would dare pull off a dirty trick of that kind. 'By the great goolies of the Adolf Hitler!' he swore, 'I'll pound that shit into wallpaper if it's him!' He rushed forward, and peered into the dirty, fly-blown little window.

To his immense relief, there was no sign of either the *Starost*'s daughter or Meier. Instead a group of tribesmen were squatting on their haunches around a low wooden table, drinking from an enamel pail of vodka, which was passed from man to man, listening intently to the sly-faced *Starost*, who was obviously explaining something to them by means of a rough sketch drawn in the dust at his feet.

Jap stared at the group in drunken bewilderment. What the hell were they sitting up for at this time of the night, listening to a lecture? Any right-thinking man was in the hay with his woman by now, and if he was of good moral character, he'd be busy slipping her a link, he told himself. That was only fair. Women liked that kind of salami-spiel. You couldn't disappoint them if you were any kind of real man. All the same, he was fascinated by the sight. In three devils' name, what could they be talking about? He screwed his head round and tried to get a better look at the sketch. He puffed out his lips in a gesture of contempt. He couldn't make head or tail of it. A long oblong with a couple of arrows drawn at each end of it. What was that shittingly well supposed to mean?

He forgot the girl he had come to make love to. He seemed hypnotized by the low drone of conversation from within, although he could not understand a single word of it. He followed the *Starost*'s every gesture, as he explained whatever he was talking about in lengthy detail, licking his dry lips in envy every time one of the tribesmen raised the pail of vodka.

And then the *Starost* began to draw a familiar shape in the dust with his dirty long finger and it was suddenly quite clear to him what this strange meeting in the middle of the night was all about. His drunkenness vanished in a flash. The *Starost* was drawing a *Schmeisser* machine pistol on the floor, with the loving attention to detail of a Rubens, shaping in one of the mighty, red-tipped breasts of the fleshy nudes the Dutch master delighted in, almost drooling in anticipation, as if he could not wait to get his skinny yellow paws on such a beautiful weapon. When he was finished, he looked up at the tribesmen's expectant faces, rapacious and menacing in the flickering candlelight. They responded as he had anticipated. They sighed with awe, and one or two of them simulated a soldier firing the machine pistol, swinging an imaginary *Schmeisser* from left to right, lips chattering like the high-pitched hiss of the weapon.

Jap needed to know no more. All thoughts of the girl had vanished now. He was stone-cold sober, aware suddenly of the wind hissing about his naked rump and the danger of his present position. Cautiously, not taking his eyes off the yellow light, he started to back to the rope ladder.

He didn't quite make it. He stumbled into one of the crude cages in which the tribesmen kept their pigeons. A dozen pigeons squawked in sudden alarm. The door flew open. Pigeons flew out in a white blur with a rattle of wings. '*Stoi*!' a hoarse voice croaked. A tribesman was staring at him, ancient rifle coming to his shoulder.

Jap was quicker off the mark. His heart thumping like a triphammer, he darted forward. His naked knee slammed into the tribesman's stomach. He gasped like the air escaping abruptly from a punctured balloon, and jack-knifed. Jap's knee rammed into his chin. He shot backwards over the wall, arms flailing wildly, screaming at the top of his voice. And then Jap was swinging down the ladder, his hands burning as he slid down, while from above him there came the sudden sounds of confusion, rage and alarm. Next moment he was pelting down the dusty street, his rump a white blur in the glowing darkness.

'What was that?' Lieutenant Haas asked in sudden fear, as the stillness of the night was broken by the first wild snap-and-crackle of rifle-fire.

'Well, it wasn't New Year fireworks, sir,' Sergeant-major Meier answered easily.

The young officer felt that familiar bunching of his arm-muscles and the tightening of his hands to claws, as if his body possessed independent volition. An uncontrollable tremor gripped his right leg. Fear overcame him once more.

Meier, standing at the head of the little six-man patrol, looked up the road as if bored; as if mysterious shots in the middle of the night were very much routine to him: something not worth mentioning.

Haas gulped and forced himself to speak, attempting to control his voice, but failing lamentably. 'What . . . what do you suggest we do, Meier?' he quavered.

Meier unslung his machine pistol and shrugged. 'You're the officer, sir. It's always the officers and gents who make the decisions in the Greater German Wehrmacht.' His tone was casual, and offensive; all the same, his keen eyes were searching the darkness for any sign of trouble. The Chinks might just be celebrating by letting off a few wild shots like they had that afternoon, he told himself. But they might be up to something else. You just couldn't trust foreigners.

'But Sergeant-major, you are a veteran – experienced—' The plea died on Haas's trembling lips.

A wild figure was pelting towards them, gasping something in what appeared to be German.

Instinctively Meier dropped to one knee and clicked off his safety.

'*Don't shoot . . . don't shoot,*' the figure yelled. '*It's me . . . me!*'

'*Freeze!*' Meier commanded, while Haas fumbled fearfully for his pistol with fingers that felt like thick, swollen sausages.

'I can't shittingly well freeze,' the running figure cried breathlessly. 'They're after me!'

'It's you — *Jap!*' Meier exclaimed, as Jap came running full-tilt into the little patrol. His eyes flashed down to the little corporal's naked lower half. 'What's this, you dirty little perverted banana-sucker? Don't tell me you got caught on the job with your skivvies down?' He threw back his head and bellowed with laughter. 'What's up? Some nasty big tribesman after yer with a sharp knife?'

Jap, his chest heaving violently, tried to control his wild

67

breathing. 'You'll be laughing on the other side of yer mug in a minute. They're after me!'

'Who?'

'The Karatski – and they're coming to attack the barn. The shits are after our weapons . . . They'd been planning it all along. That's why they got us all pissed last night.'

'The turds!' Meier cried angrily, and spinning round on the patrol, he ordered, 'All right, you farts, don't just stand there. Take up your positions. I'm going to smear those treacherous bastards all over the wallpaper when they start coming down this street.'

Lieutenant Haas suddenly woke up to his danger. Already he could hear the soft shuffle of their naked feet in the darkness. He remembered what the C.O. had said about the tribesmen's habit of emasculating their enemies, and a sudden terrifying vision of his own grotesquely mangled body flashed before his mind's eye. 'No, Sergeant-major,' he cried, 'we're too weak to stop them here. We'd better get back to the others.'

'But once they get us all in that barn . . .!' Meier began to protest.

Haas was not listening. Overcome by a great all-consuming fear, he cried, 'Come on – everyone back to the barn! *Quick*!'

And then he was running the way they had come, followed by the rest of the men. From the darkness came cries of triumph. Slugs started to howl off the walls next to Meier. He cursed, and slung his machine pistol. 'Come on, Jap, get the lead out of your butt. Shit, the C.O.'s going to rupture a gut about this!'

Behind them the tribesmen began to close in, knowing now that they had successfully sprung their trap on the Germans . . .

FIVE

'Damn it, Haas, why the devil didn't you stay in the street and stop . . .' An angry, red-faced Colonel Stuermer ducked as the first slug slammed into the open door of the barn and showered the gasping men filing through it with wood-splinters. 'All right, Haas, get inside quick! It's too late.' Stuermer crashed the door to as the first tribesmen started to come into sight, firing as they came.

He swung around at the tousled-haired, hungover mountaineers who had been wakened from their drunken sleep so rudely and were now frantically searching for their clothes and weapons, 'Get those lights!' he bellowed above the rising crescendo of the small-arms fire from outside. 'And man those windows. At the double!'

Ox-Jo didn't wait for the rest. He barrelled his way through the confused throng, and smashing the glass of the nearest window, fired a rapid burst into the gloom. There was an anguished yelp of pain, and then the tribesmen's combined fire swamped the wooden barn.

The thin planks shattered like matchwood. Bullet holes appeared everywhere. Wood splinters flew through the air. Here and there a mountaineer was hit and cried out in pain. 'Down – to the ground!' Major Greul yelled hastily.

The veterans flung themselves flat on the dirt floor. With the butts of their carbines and their sharp-bladed mountain knives they started to hack firing-holes in the base of the planks. Lying full-length, with the bullets singing over their heads only millimetres away, they began to return the enemy's fire.

Crouched behind one of the broad trestle tables, which was of thick oak and offered satisfactory protection from the tribesmen's slugs, a worried Colonel Stuermer took stock of his position hurriedly, while the snap and crackle of small-arms fire mounted in intensity.

The barn was surrounded on three sides, where it faced the street. Its fourth side was built up against a sheer rock wall. Indeed, at this moment he could feel the coldness of the stone against his own sweat-soaked shirt. Presumably their attackers thought there was no way out for them that way, since so far there had been no fire from above on that side.

But what were the tribesmen's intentions? Suddenly he spotted Jap crawling back and forth among the mess of equipment and clothing. For some reason known only to himself he was naked below the waist. 'Corporal,' he called above the frantic racket, 'over here!'

Jap crawled hurriedly to the cover of the upturned trestle table, his skinny rump moving like clockwork, with the slugs cutting the air dangerously close to it. Under other circumstances, Stuermer would have found the sight funny, but not at this particular moment. 'Jap,' he said urgently. 'You were outside just now, though God knows what you were up to, half-naked like that. No matter. What happened?'

In short chopped sentences, Jap told him what he had seen, raising his voice to almost a shout whenever the racket got too loud.

'Thank you,' Stuermer snapped when he was finished, 'All right, get off and find yourself a pair of pants, for God's sake! You'd not make a very military-looking corpse at the moment.'

Jap laughed and scuttled away to continue his search.

So that was it, Stuermer told himself. They wanted the Stormtroop's weapons to replace their own ancient pieces. They had planned the whole thing right from the start, to lull the mountaineers into a false sense of security. Now it was obvious that they were prepared to kill in order to obtain those weapons. Suddenly a very alarming thought flashed through a worried Colonel Stuermer's head. They wouldn't want those weapons destroyed, and they certainly weren't going to throw away their own lives purposelessly in all-out attack on the barn. After all, the mountaineers were trapped in the ricketty structure. There was no way out for them. So how would they obtain the precious weapons intact? The answer to that particular question made Colonel Stuermer shudder involuntarily with sudden fear. It was obvious. *They would burn them out!*

The woman, standing on the dark heights far above, lowered her night glasses, and the scarlet stab and spurt of the soundless fire-fight below vanished from the bright circles of glass.

Sergei, standing attentively at her side, her sole companion, since she had left the partisan unit forty-eight hours before, looked at her handsome face inquiringly. She said nothing.

He flashed her one of his gleaming stainless-steel smiles, his narrow youthful face lit up by the first blood-red rays of sun, which was now beginning to rise over the snowy peaks.

She became aware of his presence. 'You have done well, comrade,' she said. 'You guessed right that Bandit would do anything for weapons, even to accepting advice from Moscow's running dogs.'

'Yes, first the pigs wanted to slit my throat, and then they fed me and gave me to drink as if I was one of their own greasy selves, after I had explained about the weapons the Fritzes were bringing with them,' the young partisan said, obviously very pleased with the success of his mission to the Karatski.

'Let them enjoy their moment of triumph, Sergei. In due course, we will reckon with them. Then they will learn what kind of bill Moscow will present them with.' [1]

'And now?' Sergei asked expectantly. He had been alone with the woman from Moscow for forty-eight hours as they had wandered through the mountains. Now their mission, as far as he knew, was completed. She was a handsome woman and in spite of his stainless steel teeth, he was generally regarded by the girls of the collective farm, from which he had fled to the partisans, as not without charm. He was young, they were alone, and the sap was rising. He knew of a mountain hut where the two of them . . .

'Now,' the blonde woman cut into his fond picture of what they might do together in that lonely hut. 'Now you must go back to your unit, my dear Sergei.'

'But—'

'No buts,' she said firmly, but there was a smile on her lips as she spoke.

'And you?'

'Me?' She swung round and pointed to the far peak, gleaming a cold pink now in the rising sun. 'I have other duties.'

'Up there?' Sergei asked incredulously.

She didn't answer his question. Instead she said, her hand

[1] The woman spoke the truth. In 1946 that bill was presented, and the Karatski disappeared from history, all quarter of a million of them (author).

fumbling at her belt, as if she were in a hurry to be gone, 'Perhaps you would help me with my rucksack?'

'Yes, comrade,' Sergei said grumpily, cheering up a little at the thought that he might get a feel of her magnificent breasts as he helped her on with the sack. He bent and seized the straps. In that same instant, she pulled out her pistol and aimed it at a spot directly behind his right ear. Just as Sergei grunted and prepared to lift, she fired. The shot broke the silence of the mountain. Somewhere a startled bird flew shrieking with alarm into the still blue air. Sergei's skull shattered in a red flurry of blood and bone. He slumped over the rucksack. Calmly, completely unaffected by the murder she had just committed, the woman planted her foot in Sergei's ribs and pushed the limp body to one side in the snow. Easily she lifted the heavy rucksack and swung it over her shoulders. Without even another look at the dead boy, whose stainless-steel teeth gleamed grotesquely against the bloody snow, she turned and began her long climb to the far peak. Down below, the first fire bombs started to hit the barn.

Tinder-dry and resinous, the shattered planks started to burn. In the sudden thick choking smoke, mountaineers ran back and forth, dragging the wounded out of danger and searching around for water to extinguish the flames, while others, wreathed in smoke, tried to keep the fire-bombers at a safe distance. Meier, his broad face streaked with sweat and black stains, sprang from hole to hole, firing at every new bomber he could spot, as they darted forward, burning pitch torches in their hands, within throwing distance of the barn.

Haas, crouched in the far corner of the barn, could not move. His eyes were fixed on the body of a mountaineer, impaled on the splintered wreck of one of the trestle tables, a ghastly, mangled caricature of the man he had once been: decapitated, horrible, and totally frightening, with the blood dripping steadily from the purple hole in his neck.

Haas had been afraid many times before, but never like this. No one around him could even imagine the waves of panic-stricken, nauseating fear that flooded his body over and over again and threatened to take over his whole nervous system. Any moment, he knew, he would begin screaming. He was keeping control of himself by a mere hair's breadth. Yet he knew he had been the cause of everything. He had heard the shooting behind them that first day when they had left Cherkassy, and he hadn't reported it. He had panicked in the street, and instead of throwing a barrier across the road until the men in the barn had been alerted by the firing, he had fled, and allowed the trap to close upon the Stormtroop. Now all these good brave men were going to be burnt alive because of his cowardice. He shuddered as yet another pine-resin torch exploded with a great *whoosh* as it hit the wooden boards to his right. A mountaineer fell back, hastily beating out the flames which threatened to engulf him.

Haas swallowed and sobbed out loud, 'No ... *no!*'

Two metres away, Greul, his tunic singed and holed, his face black, paused in between shots and flashed him a look of absolute, bottomless contempt, and Haas knew he had been discovered at last. His fear had been spotted. What of his self-respect? Sick and spent, moaning aloud in self-loathing, Haas staggered across the burning room, blundering over the slumped bodies, ignoring the ricochets howling from shattered wall to wall, blindly trying to find the only man he had ever trusted, Colonel Stuermer.

Stuermer knew that he must act – and act at once. Time was running out fast for Stormtroop Edelweiss. He could surrender. But he knew what the result would be. Bandit and the tribesmen would massacre them, once they had surrendered their weapons. He had no illusions on that score. But what was he to do? He glanced around the room. He had already lost ten men and there were perhaps a dozen wounded, sheltering as best they could behind the burning tables, coughing and choking in the thick acrid smoke which was beginning to fill the barn. He had only a matter of minutes left.

'*Meier!*' he yelled above the racket.

The big NCO, his tunic ruined, to reveal singed brawny arms, scuttled across to him. 'Sir.'

'On my shoulders!' Stuermer ordered.

'What?'

'No time for explanations. Do as I order.'

Stuermer bent, and dropping his *Schmeisser*, Ox-Jo clambered on his C.O.'s back. Stuermer groaned involuntarily under the NCO's weight. But in spite of his lean figure, Stuermer possessed tremendous strength. He straightened up so that Meier's head was just beneath the wooden roof. 'Make a hole,' he ordered through gritted teeth, the veins standing out a deep blue at his temples, the sweat running down his forehead and threatening to blind him. '*Quick!*'

Meier didn't hesitate. He knew there was no time to remove the planking. He smashed his big shaven head against the planks. They snapped. He crashed his skull home once more. They gave altogether and suddenly he was breathing fresh, cold air.

'What's it like?' Stuermer called thickly. 'The rock face?'

'Shitty, sir,' Meier said, staring up at the almost perpendicular wall that rose some hundred metres above the barn. No wonder the Karatski had not bothered to post people up there. Although they were a mountain folk themselves, they hadn't thought anyone could tackle that sort of a pitch. 'I couldn't do it.'

'Could I?'

Meier hesitated for an instant. 'I think so, sir. But it'd be a shit under these conditions.'

'Good enough. Drop down. I can't carry you any longer, you Bavarian bull.'

Meier dropped lightly, for such a big man, just as Haas, his face ashen, his lips pressed tightly together to prevent them from trembling, approached his C.O.

'What is it?'

'Sir,' he blurted out, his face suddenly revealing the depth of his misery and self-loathing, 'I've let you down!'

'Nonsense,' Stuermer cut him short, his mind already full of the one way of escape left to the trapped mountaineers.

'But I have, sir. I panicked. I should have remained out there and held them off until you had a chance to get the men

outside. I'm—' he gulped before he spoke the word, 'I'm . . .
a rotten coward.'

'You are a young officer, who lost his nerve in his first action.
Now you must let me—'

'I know what you are going to do, sir. And I don't think
you've got a chance. Once they spot you attempting that
climb, they'll concentrate all their fire upon you. It stands to
reason.'

'Agreed. But we have smoke bombs. Once I'm up there—'

'But you've got to be up there first.' Again the young officer
cut him short, knowing that if Stuermer didn't accept his offer
now, tried to appease him, he would break down and sink to
the floor, a weeping abject mess.

'What do you suggest then, Haas?' Stuermer snapped,
knowing how right the boy was.

With a final effort of will, Lieutenant Haas forced himself
to say the two simple words, 'A decoy!'

A knotted ball of jangling, writhing nerves filled his lower
body. He felt as if he might wet himself at any moment. Hastily he grasped the rope, while below in the barn, Meier
steadied it. He took one last deep gasp of the acrid air and
thrust his head through the hole in the roof. Next instant he
had begun the climb to the ledge on which the rope was
anchored.

From below there came angry shouts. Slugs started to chip
the rock all around him. Something stung his cheek. Blood
spurted up hot and wet. He ignored it, concentrating now on
heaving himself upwards, trying to forget that overwhelming
fear, the knowledge that soon – very soon – hard, hot lead
would smack into the defenceless soft flesh of his back.

Young Lieutenant Haas had begun his last climb.

Stuermer heard the new salvo of shots and knew they had
spotted Haas. It was now or never. He slung the container of
smoke bombs over his shoulder and reached up to the place, a
a little covered by the barn's chimney, where Meier had broken open another exit. Easily he swung himself up and through

75

it. For an instant he knelt behind the stone chimney. Down below in the battle-littered streets, the robed figures of the tribesmen were hidden in the doorways, firing at the boy going up the steep cliff like a Bavarian mountain goat. The slugs whined off the rock in angry flurries of blue and red sparks everywhere, but he seemed to bear a charmed life. So far he hadn't been hurt.

'Good luck, boy!' Stuermer whispered under his breath, and then forgot Haas. Swinging round, still concealed by the chimney, he surveyed the almost sheer face. Then he spotted what he sought: a small indentation in the rock, which might offer him some elementary cover from the riflemen down below until he was out of range of their ancient pieces.

Taking a deep breath, he sprang from his cover and grasped the rock in his practised hands. His boots dug into a fissure. They held. His race against time had commenced.

The slug had hit him in the right shoulder. It hurt like hell. Twice he slid into the darkness of near-unconsciousness and twice he struggled up from the depths of the black stupor and kept on climbing, how, he knew not. All he knew was that he must keep on going and keep attracting their fire. 'Nightmare,' he told himself, 'I'm having a nightmare. It's not true. It's not happening to me. I'm not crawling up a cliff face I would never have tackled in reality. I'm not wounded – and I'm not going to fall to my death in a moment. Nightmare!'

The slugs continued to whine off the rock all around him. He was hit again. He hardly felt the pain. He was half way up now. Two or three metres away, wavering in the red mist in front of his eyes now, he saw a ledge. There he would rest. Yes, there he would rest! He crawled on, the bullets striking the stone in furious flurries of angry red sparks. He did not hear them. He did not hear the angry cries from below. Now he heard nothing, felt nothing. His sole concern was on keeping going until he reached that ledge.

He hooked his bleeding, torn fingers into the rock, his feet automatically seeking for a toe-hold. With a grunt, he levered himself upwards and onto it.

For an instant the fog which had swamped his mind lifted. He saw the burning barn below, the angry upturned faces, heard the whine of the bullets off the rock and knew fear for the last time. He was alone and going to die – and he was only eighteen; he had never even known a woman. Then the deadening fog swept over him again and the fear vanished.

Slowly, infinitely slowly, he raised himself on the ledge to his full height so that he presented a target which would anger them, keep them firing, would draw their attention from Colonel Stuermer. The bullets increased in volume. The tribesmen even forgot the fire-bombs in their anger. Now all their efforts were concentrated on bringing down the man who taunted them thus.

A burst struck the rock near his head. The chips showered his face. He felt the pain momentarily. He laughed crazily. 'Miss—' he began, just as the volley of rifle fire ripped open his stomach. He felt nothing. There was no fear now. There was only a vast, heedless indifference. His knees started to fold beneath him. He did not try to stop the movement, although he knew quite clearly he would fall if he didn't. Like a stone he fell. He made no sound. That final scream of unbearable agony never passed his lips. He hit the ground with a dull sickening thud. His body bounced up again with the impact, and in that instant before his spine snapped like a rotten twig and he died, Lieutenant Haas was glad.

Stuermer heard the crash of the body hitting the ground and felt the grey bitterness of defeat; he could almost taste its sourness. So young, and dead already. Then he thought of the others and forced out of his mind the bitter lassitude which had threatened to overcome him. He must save the Stormtroop!

He fought his way up the sheer rock face, his muscles afire, the breath rasping in great gulping inhalations into his oxygen-starved lungs, keeping up an impossible pace, knowing that every second counted now. On and on. A brutal gasping agony. He was nearly there now. Still they hadn't discovered him. He ripped off his nails as his right hand sought and failed to find a

77

purchase on a slab of rock that gave way beneath his desperate fingers. He tried again, ignoring the pain in his hand, which made him want to scream out loud. He found a hold. He climbed on. Below, the fire bombs were hissing through the air again. He could hear the fierce crackle of the burning barn.

He reached the ledge. His bleeding fingers dug into the earth until they were locked in solid rock. He could not afford to fall now. He found a toe-hold and raised himself. He gasped with surprise. Twenty metres away a man was sitting, long rifle between his knees, with his back towards Stuermer, smoking a cigarette calmly, as if the brutal murder taking place below was happening on another planet.

Every movement as smooth and controlled as possible, Stuermer wormed his way over the edge of the cliff. Praying that the man wouldn't hear him, grateful for the wind that blew up on the top and drowned some of his movements, he started to crawl towards the unsuspecting sentry. Fifteen metres . . . ten metres . . . Still the sentry didn't hear him . . . Five metres. With his good hand, Stuermer freed the mountain knife at his waist . . . three metres. The man *must* hear him now!

Suddenly Stuermer saw the sentry's right shoulder move. He tensed. The skinny yellow claw which gripped the long rifle tightened. The man started to turn. Stuermer dived forward, knife upraised. The two of them crashed together and the impact flung the man to the ground. Stuermer's knife flashed. He grunted. The sentry howled and the breath left him in a violent, convulsive exhalation. Stuermer heard the thud of his knife-hilt striking home against the ribs. He plunged it in once again and the sentry's crazy writhings ceased. He went limp. He was dead!

For a moment the two of them, the dead and quick, lay there, clasped together like spent lovers. Then Stuermer pushed the dead man away and sprang to his feet, the bloody knife clattering to the rock. He doubled back to the edge of the cliff. He flung the first smoke-bomb over. It exploded with a soft plop. Almost immediately thick white smoke streamed from it. Another followed. In seconds the attacking tribesmen vanished from view. Stuermer did not waste another second. With frantic, bleeding fingers he started to play out the rope . . .

Section Three

THE BATTLE FOR A PASS

ONE

He was smaller than most of them had imagined, fatter too, and with that half smile on his thick sensual lips they could understand why the Americans called him, with such disrespect, 'Uncle Joe'. Yet there was no denying the power of the man. Even the simple gesture of stuffing a cigarette into his hooked pipe, while the most powerful officers in the Red Army waited for him to speak, revealed the might this pock-marked Georgian possessed.

Finally he was finished and began to explain the reason for their hurried summons from the Southern Front. 'Comrades,' he said, and his Georgian accent was very evident, 'I don't need to tell you that the Red Army has suffered a very severe reverse on the Southern Front. Our troops have been driven back across the Kuban and into the Caucasus.'

The generals lowered their gazes. Were heads going to roll? Was that the reason they had been called to Moscow? Siberia and the murderous labour camps of the snow wilderness – was that where they were heading after they left here?

'I don't need to tell you, either, what the loss of the Caucasus would mean for us. We could afford the loss of the oil. But if Turkey entered the war on the German side as a result of that loss . . .' The little dictator shrugged. 'Well, I need to say no more, do I, comrades?'

There was a hasty murmur of agreement.

Josef Stalin puffed almost happily at his hooked pipe, his avuncular face wreathed in blue smoke, as if he didn't have a care in the world.

In the pause, Aleksandr Poskrebyshev, Stalin's sinister hunchbacked secretary, hobbled from general to general pouring eau de cologne on their outstretched hands. Gratefully the generals dabbed the cologne on their foreheads in the Soviet fashion – whether because of the heat in the room or whether on account of their fears about what might be coming, known only to themselves. 'Old Leather Face', as they called the dictator behind his back, watched them with something akin to amusement in his dark brown eyes.

Finally Stalin broke the heavy silence. 'You understand our problem then, comrades and that it is imperative that we hold the Germans back when they attack – and our Intelligence tells us that they will attack soon. Now in what direction will they attack?' He answered his own question, as the silent generals had expected him to. 'The Fritzes' alternatives are limited, due to the terrain. Down the valley of the Kuban, swing south to – say – Suchumi and then along the coastal littoral of the Black Sea south-east and into the Caucasus.'

There was a murmur of agreement from the generals and Colonel-General Kozlov, the senior officer present, said, 'That is what we think, Comrade Stalin. The *Stavka* [1] is of the same opinion.'

'Is that so, Comrade Kozlov?' Stalin said with deceptive softness. 'And you have made your dispositions accordingly, I presume?'

'Yes, Comrade Stalin,' said Kozlov, a broad-chested bear of a man, whose tight-fitting tunic, with its heavy gold epaulettes, was bright with the battle ribbons of forty years of campaigning. 'We have the mass of three armies, plus several independent artillery and armoured corps, packed into the bottle-neck, from which they must emerge on the Black Sea coast.'

'I see. Therefore you have put all your eggs in one basket, Comrade Colonel-General,' Stalin said, his voice still very low.

Kozlov flushed. 'I don't quite understand, Comrade Stalin—' he began.

'And because of it you deserve a kick up your damn stupid kulak arse!' Stalin exploded, cutting into his words brutally. 'Do you think the Fritzes are fool enough not to realize that we will be waiting for them once they move along the Black Sea coast? It is as if they are giving us a written invitation to be ready to receive them there. No, Kozlov, the Fritz generals

[1] The Soviet Supreme High Command.

are not as mad as their master! They do not play foolish games like that.'

Kozlov's professional pride was hurt. 'Comrade Stalin, aerial reconnaissance shows, however, that the Germans are massing their forces above the Black Sea coast. Besides, how else can they get out of the Kuban Basin?'

By way of an answer, Stalin clicked his fingers. The hunchback hobbled over to him, bearing the map, as if he could read his master's mind. He spread it, uncommanded, across the great marble table at which the Czars had once signed their papers.

Stalin rapped it with his pipe. 'Here, Comrade Generals, *here*!'

Kozlov looked at the dictator's pock-marked face, as if he had gone out of his mind. 'But Comrade Stalin,' he objected, 'those are the high mountains. Even in summer they are virtually unsurmountable.'

'Did they never teach you about Hannibal in that academy to which we sent you to learn to read and write?' Stalin sneered.

'Hannibal did not possess armour. Nor did he have to transport heavy shells and rations for half a million men,' Kozlov said, knowing now he was not only risking his command, but also his neck.

'But he crossed the Alps in the dead of winter and kicked the Romans up their surprised arses, just as the Fritzes might well do to you, if I were not here to protect you from your own foolishness.' Stalin ignored the looks on his generals' faces. He had broken their power in '37. Those who had survived the Army purges were yes-men; he knew he could do with them what he wished. They were all deadly afraid of him, although they had the largest army in the world under their command. 'I want each army to relinquish one corps and transfer it to the rear of the mountains. I want armour and artillery too. You will say that you cannot afford to lose the troops. But you must! You must make do with what you have left.'

'Comrade Stalin.' It was Lieutenant-General Kerst, as precise and as methodical as the Germans whom he fought and from whose country his own forefathers had emigrated to

Russia. 'What indication have you that the Germans might attempt to cross the mountains?' The voice was quiet and respectful, but there was iron in it all the same.

'This. For the last three days a unit of the German High Alpine Corps has been pushing from Cherkassy up into the mountains. It is obvious that they are some kind of reconnaissance party for a large group to follow. Once the Alpine Corps has traversed the mountains, what is to stop the rest from following?'

Now the generals began to forget their initial disbelief; there was the dawning of respect on their hard wooden faces. But General Kerst was not absolutely convinced. 'One reconnaissance party, with all due respect, Comrade Stalin, does not mean more than that there is a reconnaissance party in the area.' He shrugged slightly. 'There could be a good half dozen reasons for their presence there.' There was a murmur of agreement from the others.

'You could be right, Kerst, save for one thing – our agent reports that they are equipped to climb the highest peak. That, for my poor humble self,' he added cynically, 'is proof enough.'

Still the methodical German was not convinced. 'And of what calibre is this agent? What does he know of climbing?'

'Not *he*, Comrade Kerst, but *she*,' Stalin said, pleased that he could spring his surprise on them.

'*She?*'

'Yes, my dear comrade, no other than Comrade Roswitha Mikhailovna! *Now* are you convinced?'

They didn't need to answer his question. The looks of awe on their faces told him all he wished to know; they were convinced all right. 'Now then,' he said briskly, leaning forward across the great table, 'this is what we are going to do . . .'

TWO

Roswitha Mikhailovna had been exactly ten years old when the Russian Revolution had broken out in 1917. It had changed her whole world. Her father, a humble peasant, had been murdered by the Whites, and her mother had gone off with one of the wandering bands of soldier-bandits, which were constantly passing through their miserable village. She had never returned.

In 1920, after three years of living off the land, trying to feed herself as best she could in a starving countryside, fighting off the constant demands of the men of all races and all political persuasions, who tried to go to bed with the handsome blonde virgin, she finally landed in an orphanage in Moscow as a 'ward of the state'.

She had spent her next ten years in such institutions, making up for her lost schooling, developing her magnificent body in order to achieve her aim – the qualification of Master of Sport and the teaching job that went with it. The killing routine of the training camps – the six o'clock bugle, followed by Swedish drill before breakfast, the hours in the gym, the long afternoons of basketball, the para-military training – had meant nothing to her. Where many of her male colleagues were exhausted, glassy-eyed and lathered in sweat, she was still fresh, bright-eyed and eager for more.

In the summer of 1930, just after graduation, she accepted the invitation of a group of male students to accompany them on a climb in the Caucasus mountains. It was to be her job to take care of the ground organization of the climbs, preparing the routine pre-climb form with its details of the number of climbers, their target, estimated time-of-return, etc, and arranging the usual welcome ceremony-address by the local camp commandant, presentation of flowers for a successful climb and so on. In essence, she was going to have a rest after the long gruelling task of obtaining her Master of Sport degree.

But after the first week of inactivity and boredom, she had asked on sudden impulse, whether she could go along on a climb. Later, much later, she had reasoned that fate had willed her to go along to discover at whatever cost – a fall, an accident, even death – what made a puny mortal tackle the magnificent peaks of the majestic, silent mountains.

After that first climb, as rough, unprofessional and sometimes frightening as it was, she had seen the mountains no longer as remote sights which filled her with awe and affection. Instead, they had become the walls of enemy cities, the castles of the aristocracy, the fortresses of the reactionaries, the enemies of the Soviet State to be attacked and stormed. At that moment her sense of awe had vanished forever to be replaced by a violent, almost sexual, desire to conquer.

At the end of that climb, the senior student, who had been the leader of the climb, had spat out a mouthful of sunflower seeds, his bronzed face a mixture of awe and dislike, and said: 'Roswitha, you have determination and talent. I think our mountains better look out with you around.'

'Thank you, comrade,' she had answered, pleased with herself, forgetting her bloody knees and aching shoulder muscles. 'It was very instructive.'

'But remember one thing, Roswitha,' he had added softly, 'the mountains have to be loved too.'

But Roswitha Mikhailovna had no longer been listening . . .

From 1930 onwards, she had spent every vacation tackling ever-new climbs, saving every penny of her teacher's salary to travel all over the Soviet Union to her targets. The newspapers started to notice her. *Pravda* called her 'the new Soviet Woman'. *Trud* said she was a 'model for all our female comrades'. Her climbing motto: *'Nada vitserapat'* – 'never give in' became famous throughout the Soviet Union.

By 1935 Roswitha Mikhailovna had become one of the Soviet Union's best-known women, had been given a sinecure at Moscow University, and had even been granted the great honour of being received by Comrade Stalin himself, who publicly had awarded her the Order of the Red Star and privately remarked to his fellow Georgian Beria, head of the

Secret Police, 'Lavrenti Pavlovich, I could think of a better occupation for that particular piece of female flesh—'

'Yes,' the Secret Police Chief, who was known for his sexual exploits, had agreed: 'On her back with her legs spread!'

'Only with those muscles, *I think she'd squeeze me to death!*' And the two old lechers had burst into ribald laughter.

But Roswitha Mikhailovna was no lesbian. Neither was she a blue-stocking. She liked men and she liked pretty clothes. She thought of herself as a feminist: a patriotic, loyal Russian, who owed everything to the Soviet State, which allowed her to do the thing she loved most, climb mountains; but who at the same time wanted herself to be seen as an example to the many millions of Russian women who had been downtrodden for centuries by men who had gone to bed on their honeymoon night, drunk, satiated from the attentions of the whores, and armed with a knout [1] to tame the new bride.

Now she climbed, this amazing, ambitious woman, who had spent the last three months behind the German lines, risking her neck time and time again to help prevent the enemy breaking out of the Kuban valley into the Caucasus. The going was tough. It did not worry her. Over the mountain lay a coverlet of pale clouds, closely knit and swirling. The sun had vanished too and the rocks looked bluish and lifeless. She knew that snow was on the way. But neither the difficulty of the ascent nor the prospect of bad weather dismayed her, as she struggled ever upwards. She was going back to her friends, and that knowledge lent strength and purpose to her long elegant legs.

The wind rose. It whistled a dirge across the face of the rock. The dirty white clouds were directly above her now and they were becoming more leaden in appearance by the second. It started to snow: thin weak flakes at first, but swiftly growing in strength. She pulled down her goggles with a gloved hand, knowing instinctively they would be clogged up within minutes. Still she pressed on determinedly, hardly able to wait until she was with them again, feeling an almost sexual longing for them, but dismissing the feeling at once as perverse.

As she ploughed through the snow, her agile mind ran over

[1] Russian whip.

the events of the last few days. She had hated killing Sergei, but it was better that one should suffer death than thousands. A careless word on his part might well have revealed their presence in the mountains. He had to go. For it was certain that the Germans would send another patrol into the mountains, if only to discover what had happened at Chursuk; and it was not too difficult to reason that that patrol might press on further to continue their attempt to find a route through the mountains down into the great plain below. Once the Germans discovered just how weak the Russian defences were, they would cross the mountains in their thousands into the Caucasus beyond. Until Comrade Stalin was ready for them – and she was sure that he would heed her warning – she had to hold the mountains. Thus she pushed on, her mind full of the problems of defence.

'*Stoi?*' the high-pitched challenge came from the middle of nowhere, echoing and re-echoing around .the circle of mountain peaks.

Roswitha Mikhailovna halted. She whipped off her goggles and narrowing her eyes against the flying snowflakes, peered around in the grey gloom. She could see nothing. She licked her snow-dry cracked lips. 'Where are you?' she called, high and harsh.

'*Stoi?*' the voice demanded again.

Now she located it. It came from beneath a snow-heavy overhang to her right. She swung round and called happily, 'Better not shout too loud. Or you'll have that lot of snow down upon you.'

'It's you!' the voice was no longer harsh.

'Who did you expect – *Hitler?*' she said in high good humour.

'*Boshe Moi!*' A white-clad bulky figure clad in a snowsuit detached itself from the cover of the overhang and waddled with difficulty across the fresh snow, slinging a rifle as it did so.

Roswitha waited there, her arms outspread.

The other flung back the fur hood. A round youthful face, full of strength and character, under the carefully plucked dark eyebrows, came into view. '*Lydia!*' Roswitha cried happily and embraced the other woman joyfully, kissing her time and time again in the Russian fashion. At last she was back with her own kind again.

THREE

It was the next morning.

Roswitha stood at the entrance to the caves surveying the terrain below, her keen gaze sweeping the smooth gleaming white surface of the mountains, checking for the enemy, but at the same time enjoying the view. How beautiful the great curved sweep of the valley was, cradled in the embrace of the high mountains and falling away gently to the south!

She turned and stared at the mountain, gleaming pink and pure in the dawn light. One day, she promised herself, she would conquer it too. Those twin peaks would be hers. A warm feeling swept through her body, as she visualized surmounting those peaks which looked so like the breasts of some proud young virgin, as yet unconquered by the importuning male. The next moment she dismissed the feeling as decadent and unworthy of a feminist, who did not succumb to the foolishness of the general run of womanhood. Taking a deep breath of pure mountain air, she thrust back the canvas cover to the main entrance to the cave system and for an instant surveyed her still sleeping troop, their bodies wrapped in their heavy down sleeping bags, which rose and fell rhythmically as the women enjoyed the last moments of their time free of war.

She smiled, her face full of compassion and pride. They had laughed at her in Moscow when she had offered them her militia unit back in July 1941. What good were women, they had asked contemptuously, save as nurses, or perhaps snipers? 'Give me and my girls a chance,' she had pleaded. In the end, grateful for anyone capable of carrying and firing a rifle, they had; and she had proved just what her girls could do. On the coldest night of the year in January 1942, when sentries froze to death at their post, she and her girls had climbed the ramparts of the German-held fortress outside beleaguered Leningrad, slaughtered the divisional commander and his staff who were billeted there, and escaped without a single casualty.

The exploit had occasioned sensational headlines in the Soviet Press. But it had been nothing in comparison with her girls' bold attempt to break through the German Volga front by scaling the heights and assassinating the commander of the German Sixth Army. That attempt had failed. But it had made the Fritzes so insecure that they had begun to see partisans everywhere. Stalin himself had ordered the girls to be paraded through Moscow, and to be received and heaped with decorations at the Kremlin. The legend of the 'Red Ravens', as the popular press called them due to their myriad decorations, had been born. Now no one, even the most anti-feminist general in the *Stavka*, dare denigrate her girls. The Red Ravens were a unit to be reckoned with, even if they did wear skirts when they were not in line. As Stalin himself had told the Russian people, 'Wherever the front is the hottest, comrades, you will find my bold and beautiful Red Ravens.' It had been high praise indeed, and Roswitha Mikhailovna was determined to live up to it.

Taking out her whistle, she blew three shrill blasts. The girls awoke at once like the veterans they were, who knew that in an emergency immediate obedience to a command might well mean the difference between life and death. Leaping out of their sleeping bags, already fully clad save for their mountaineering boots, they stood stiffly to attention, staring rigidly to the front, as if they were standing on some home-front parade ground, waiting to be inspected by Marshal Voroshilov himself.[1]

She smiled and snapped, 'Stand at ease, comrades – and good morning.'

'Good morning, Comrade Captain,' they answered.

'We will have a conference in—' she checked her cheap wristwatch – 'exactly thirty minutes. There are things I need to explain to you.' She smiled at the dark-haired Lydia, who had welcomed her the day before and joked, 'And for goodness

[1] Commander-in-Chief, Red Army.

92

sake, Lydia, let your hair down. At the moment you look like –
er – one of *those*.'

Lydia flushed and the others laughed. They all knew what
'those' were. After all, most of the hardline anti-feminists of
the *Stavka* thought that this was what the Red Ravens were all
about. Giggling they set about preparing the morning soup and
tea.

They crowded around her in the main gallery of the cave
system, their young handsome bodies shapeless in their thick,
heavily wadded jackets and coarse serge mountain pants. To
Roswitha waiting to brief them, they looked no different than
their male comrades of the Red Army. Naturally they would
fight and die like the men, but they could not be ordered to do
things like their male comrades. They had to have their orders
explained to them.

'Comrades,' she commenced, 'I have been on a long and not
very pleasant mission. Like you, living under these hard conditions, I would like a rest. I would like to ensure you have a
rest too.'

'No, no,' they protested, as loyal as ever. 'We need no rest.
We will perform our duty however tired and cold we may be.'

'Thank you, comrades,' she said, visibly moved, knowing
how hard their lives had been these last six weeks in the high
mountains. 'I knew I could rely upon you – no, more, that
Mother Russia could rely upon you – at this grave hour, when
everything is balanced on a knife's edge.'

Sergeant Lanya Lermintov, a raw-boned woman in her early
thirties, whose jet-black hair was cropped as short as any
soldier's and who before the war had been – like most of the
Red Ravens – one of Russia's best amateur rock-climbers, spat
in the dust of the cave and growled: 'Comrade Captain, I'll
stay up here till hell freezes, if it will let me get my paws on a
Fritz.' She raised her hard, calloused, ham-like hands. 'And I
can promise you, it won't be a night of love I'll offer him.' She
spat contemptuously once again.

The others laughed and Roswitha joined in dutifully. Sergeant Lermintov was always good for a joke or the apt com-

ment which could defuse any potentially explosive situation. 'Yes, I could well imagine you would have other things in mind than the – er procreation of the species.'

Again the girls laughed, and Roswitha told herself what a happy crowd they were, working together as a team, without the usual bickering of the average woman living in close proximity with another female, where the unauthorized borrowing of a simple hairpin might lead to a major quarrel complete with slanging match and hair-pulling. Her Red Ravens were not like that. One day the whole of womanhood might well be like them, freed from the domestic silliness of the average woman's life.

'Now, comrades, it is clear that we are very thin on the ground,' she went on. 'But you all know why. Our male comrades are needed for the fighting front and our generals – or some of them – have not seen the danger to our rear presented by the mountains. Good. So,' she shrugged, 'it is up to us to stop a whole German mountain corps – fifty Red Ravens against twenty thousand Fritzes.'

'Many enemies, much honour,' Lydia said. She was proud of her classical education at the University of Moscow and was given to quotes from the half-dozen languages she spoke. 'German expression,' she added for their enlightenment.

'Agreed,' Roswitha said. 'But we must realize our weaknesses. We cannot do everything with the handful of people available. We have to take certain calculated risks.'

'Such as?' one of the girls asked.

'Such as this.' Swiftly and expertly she did a quick sketch in the frozen dust of the cave's floor. 'Here – the pass,' she said. 'Here – Elbrus House. Through the pass everyone trying to cross the mountains must come, and from the House the whole range can be covered, at least at this time of the year. Now, my plan is that we leave a small group of Red Ravens at the pass. The rest of the unit should take up position at Elbrus House ready to move to any hot spot.'

'How many at the pass?' Sergeant Lermintov asked.

'We can't afford more than a dozen.'

'Far too few,' the sergeant growled in her deep voice.

'Couldn't hold the pass against a determined Fritz attack. Request permission to volunteer for command of that particular group?'

Roswitha shook her head, half amused, half moved by the big woman's offer. 'All right, Sergeant, it's yours.'

'Do I have your permission too to pick my own people, Comrade Captain?'

'You do.'

Sergeant Lermintov looked across at the pretty dark-haired Lydia, knowingly. Hurriedly Roswitha shook her head and pushed on. 'Now, as Sergeant Lermintov has just said, we cannot hold the pass against any serious Fritz attack with a dozen Red Ravens. For that reason, while you slept I asked for air.'

'Air?' they echoed.

She beamed at them, a warm feeling flooding her body as she did so. 'Yes, the *Stavka* has promised me a permanent patrol over the pass – one whole squadron of Stormoviks.'

'*Stormoviks*,' Sergeant Lermintov cried excitedly, 'that'll make the Fritzes shit their breeches ...'

The Red Ravens broke down at the words and giggled like a lot of silly schoolgirls. It was the last time that most of them would giggle in this lifetime.

FOUR

'Rata, sir! Meier, at the head of the long column toiling upwards through the snow towards the pass, yelled urgently.

'Everyone down!' Stuermer ordered.

On all sides the mountaineers, their weariness forgotten now in the urgency of this moment, flung themselves into the snow, as the sound of the little spotter plane's engine grew ever louder.

Crouched behind a rock, gloved hand shading his face so that its whiteness didn't give his position away, Colonel Stuermer followed the progress of the little wooden biplane as it curved leisurely over the pass and started to level out. On the sledges the wounded stirred uneasily at the new noise and he called sharply, 'Remain where you are – there is no danger!'

The Rata had levelled out. Now it was coming in from the east, trailing a black shadow behind it over the gleaming surface of the snow. It took its time and Stuermer could guess what the pilot, a dark blob behind the gleaming egg of the cockpit perspex, was doing: he was looking to left and right, searching the white carpet of snow – *for them*!

He caught his breath involuntarily, and froze. The Rata, its engine sounding like some ancient sewing machine, was flying straight down the trail from the pass. Now everything depended on the men of Edelweiss remaining perfectly still. In their white snowsuits they would be hard to see, especially from a moving object. With a bit of luck they would get away with it.

The noise of the engine grew ever louder. The Rata was almost above them now. Lying everywhere in the snow, the mountaineers tensed, their faces pressed into the snow, their hearts pounding furiously. And then the spotter plane was above them and Sergeant Hackebeil, who had been badly wounded in the head during the attack on the barn and who had been barely coherent since then, had staggered from his sledge, trailing bandages behind, crying weakly, 'They're gonna bomb us . . . The bastards are going to bomb us . . .'

'*Get that man!*' Stuermer yelled.

Jap was up and running. Diving low, he tackled the crazily staggering NCO and flung him to the ground, holding him there till his struggling, protesting body grew limp again, while the sound of the Rata's motor grew fainter as it disappeared behind a peak.

'Stay where you are!' Stuermer commanded. 'Not a move. He might come—'

The words died on the big colonel's lips. The Rata had emerged from behind the glistening peak, a harsh black against the bright blue of the sky. Now the spotter plane was coming in at tree-top height, its engine barely above stalling speed. Instinctively Stuermer knew they had been spotted.

There was no use attempting to hide any more. 'Independent fire!' he ordered urgently. 'Knock the bastard out of the sky!'

The mountaineers needed no further urging. They all knew what it might mean if the pilot reported his sighting back to the Red HQ. Everywhere they sprang from the snow, fumbling with their carbines as they did so.

Ox-Jo let fly with a futile burst of machine-pistol fire. The tracer zipped by the plane harmlessly. Greul, standing as if he were back on the ranges, one hand behind his back in the classic stance of the pistol marksman, took aim carefully and fired. The perspex shattered into a gleaming spider's web. The little Rata seemed to fall from the sky, as the blinded pilot fought with the controls.

'You've got him, sir,' the words sprang up from half a dozen gleeful throats to die the next instant, as the pilot somehow regained control of the spotter plane and, flying blind, speed increasing at every moment, fled for the safety of the high peaks.

'For God's sake don't let him get away!' Stuermer cried furiously above the roar of the plane's engine.

The men opened up again. Tracer slit the blue sky angrily after the speeding plane. But already it was too late. The Russian pilot banked to the right, leaving the angry tracer hissing harmlessly into nothing. A moment later the Rata had vanished behind the nearest rock wall and the firing started to die away. Suddenly there was no sound save the steady throb of the motor in the east, becoming fainter by the second.

Greul stamped across to where a red-faced, angry Stuermer stared into the sky. 'Well?' he demanded.

'Well what?'

Greul indicated the spot where the Rata had disappeared. 'I'm sure I don't have to tell you, sir, that that plane spells trouble for us.'

'You don't, Major Greul,' Stuermer answered icily, turning his attention to his arrogant second-in-command. 'So?'

'So, sir, assuming that the Rata is an indication that we shall soon be receiving visitors, what are we to do about them?' He indicated the wounded lying on the makeshift sledges.

Stuermer knew exactly what Major Greul meant, but it was something he did not even want to think about. He played stupid. 'What do you mean, Greul?'

'I mean sir, that one can't made an omelette—'

'—without breaking eggs,' Stuermer interrupted him angrily, 'I know your favourite motto, Greul. Come to the point.'

Greul flushed. 'In this kind of country, we should be pretty safe against aerial attack. With five or ten seconds' notice the men could be up the rock walls on either side and out of harm's way. We are safe as long as we are in a position to disperse swiftly. But not with those wounded.'

Greul had expressed what he had not dared even to think about, yet Stuermer was still shocked. 'But we can't abandon the wounded, Greul!' he cried. 'They are our comrades and our responsibility.'

'The decision is yours, sir,' Greul replied. 'It is either the wounded or us – and the success of our mission.' With that he turned and stumped back through the snow, leaving Stuermer standing there, his shoulders bowed, his face stricken with grief.

The dive-bombers appeared suddenly on the blood-red horizon. For one long moment they seemed to hover there, the red ball of the sun behind them.

Stuermer watched them through his binoculars, horror-stricken. They were Stormoviks, Russian dive-bombers, and they were preparing to come in with the sun behind them. It was the usual tactic: a means of blinding any gunner attempting to stop them. Standing next to him, his glasses focussed on the sinister black hawks of planes hovering on the horizon, Major Greul said quietly: 'Well, sir?'

Stuermer knew they had only a matter of moments. Could they fight the dive-bombers off? Even as he asked himself the question, he knew the answer. *No!* Their sole heavy weapons were the machine guns. But could he sacrifice the wounded like that? His face revealed the agony of decision.

Greul said, 'Time is running out, sir.'

'I know, for God's sake, I *know*!' Stuermer exploded. 'But the wounded, what can I do about the wounded?'

'Nothing, sir – and here they come.' He lowered his glasses as the black hawks sped from the horizon, growing larger by the instant.

'All right . . . all right,' Stuermer sobbed. 'Tell the men to get up on the rock wall!'

Greul did not hesitate. 'Up the rock . . . up the rock . . . *at the double!*' he yelled above the frightening roar of the approaching dive-bombers.

The mountaineers broke at once. Like human flies, weapons slung over their shoulders, they started to scale the almost sheer walls on both sides of the snow-bound mountain track. Stuermer hesitated, his face contorted with horror at the knowledge of what was soon to come. Greul grabbed him roughly by the arm. 'Come on . . . come on, Colonel. There is nothing you can do!' He broke into a run, dragging the reluctant Stuermer with him.

As they ran by the sledge which bore the dying Sergeant Hackebeil, the NCO raised himself painfully and croaked, 'The best of luck, sir. *Berg Heil!*' he gave the mountaineer's greeting and fell back exhausted to wait for the inevitable.

Stuermer sobbed and staggered on, knowing that he would not forget the look in the dying man's eyes for as long as he lived.

The squadron commander jiggled his wings. Abruptly he dropped out of the hard blue sky. At four hundred kilometres an hour, sirens howling, he hurtled for the ground. Behind him one after another the Stormoviks peeled off and did the same. Watching them from the relative safety of the rock wall, the mountaineers stared wide-eyed at the diving planes which seemed to threaten to smash into the ground at any moment.

Just when it seemed the leader would not make it, he levelled off. From their hiding place they could see quite clearly his pale blur of a face and the great red crosses on the Stormovik's side. The dive-bomber shuddered violently. Tiny deadly black eggs tumbled wildly from its belly. Behind the almost stationary Stormovik, plane after plane levelled off and discharged their bombs too.

Just as the first stick exploded with an ear-splitting crash, Stuermer caught one last glimpse of the men trapped below on their sledges, their faces contorted with fear and horror. Then his world was swamped in furious sound, drowning the screams of the dying men ...

The bombers had gone now, winging their triumphant way to the east, leaving behind them only dead mountaineers. Silently, his head bared, his eyes filled with tears of compassion and shame, Colonel Stuermer wandered in a daze through the shattered sledges: a jumbled mass of twisted weapons, smashed wood and severed limbs, already beginning, in the cold mountain air, to settle into a pool of congealing blood.

'Sir.'

Slowly Stuermer turned round. It was Ox-Jo. In his big hand he held a canteen. 'A drink sir. The last of the *Enzian*,' [1] he said, his voice unusually soft for him.

Numbly Colonel Stuermer shook his head.

'It'll do you good, sir. Put—' the words faltered to nothing, as the NCO realized that they were having no effect. He put the canteen away and said, his voice heavy and without its usual bite, 'Volunteers to bury the dead!'

Thirty minutes later, they began their progress up the Pass once more, leaving behind them fourteen rough mounds of earth and stone already beginning to be covered by the new snow. Colonel Stuermer did not look back. He couldn't.

FIVE

Sergeant Lermintov swept the ground below with her glasses, ignoring her cramped leg muscles and the stiffness in her arms. She had held the same position for nearly an hour now – ever

[1] A Bavarian and Austrian mountain drink.

since dawn when she had begun to search the area beyond the pass for any sign that the Fritzes had survived the bombing of the previous day. For Comrade Captain Mikhailovna had informed her by radio that what appeared to be another German patrol was on its way into the high mountains.

Now the sun, rime-ringed and a pale, luminous yellow after the night's fresh snow, had appeared behind the towering buttressed giant of the Elbrus and was casting long black shadows, which raced like live things across the gleaming white surface below. Everything was outlined against it a harsh stark black. Lermintov adjusted the focus of her glasses and swept the area to the right of the track which led up to the pass. She had covered the same terrain only ten minutes before. Then it had been empty. Now things had changed. From that direction came the faint shrill wheep of a whistle.

For what seemed a long time, the cropped-haired woman sergeant, lying among the snow-covered boulders, her brow creased in a puzzled frown, tried to work out the reason for this strange alien sound among the white mountain wilderness.

Then she had it. Tiny dark figures were advancing with the slow, measured movements of men ploughing through deep snow. She felt a thrill of sudden fear, but dismissed the feeling the next instant. Raising herself a little from her hiding place, she started to count them.

It wasn't easy. The tiny figures, startlingly black against the ascending sun, continually slipped into the shadows cast by the great boulders which littered the slope below, and disappeared from sight. But in the end she had it. Nearly thirty of them, spread out in a line about a kilometre in length, in its centre a man directing them forward by means of an alpenstock – an officer, probably. Thirty against a dozen women. For a moment she lay there, considering the odds watching the snail-like relentlessness with which the Fritzes advanced up the slope, knowing that inevitably they and her own force would clash. Then she remembered how well sited her own position was, and just how loyal and brave the Red Ravens were. Encouraged, she slipped out of her hiding place and started to steal back to the caves. It was a badly timed move. Because of it she missed the second force – another thirty men – moving in from the left flank.

She pushed back the canvas which covered the entrance to the caves.

'Anything wrong, Comrade Sergeant?' one of the girls asked, alarmed by the look on her broad masculine face.

Sergeant Lermintov pulled herself together. She was ten years older than her girls; she must not alarm them. 'Not much,' she said casually, taking out one of the long ration cigarettes, biting off the paper mouthpiece and lighting it with demonstrative casualness. 'I've just seen a bunch of Fritzes out there.' She breathed out a stream of blue smoke, her eyes wrinkled up as she did so.

'Fritzes?'

'Yes, perhaps thirty of them. They are spread out like fleas on a poodle's back. Easy meat for us to pick them off. Listen,' she continued more urgently. 'We have nothing to fear. We are in an excellent position up here. We have the heights and there is no way in hell that they can get past us. They might have the superior numbers, but we have the advantage of the dug-in position. Now then, don't look so glum, my beautiful Red Ravens. We're going to give those Fritzes a bloody nose – a very bloody one. *Come on*!'

The Fritzes, more closely bunched now as they came closer to the pass, were less than half a kilometre away. Sergeant Lermintov tucked the stock of her sniper's rifle deep into the hollow formed by her cheek and shoulder. The time had come to stop them. All around her the Red Ravens waited tensely. She swung the rifle round. An NCO came into the round glittering eye of the sight. She watched the Fritz blow his whistle and heard the noise it made echo mournfully down the snowbound valley like the wailing of some lost bird. She sucked in her breath and in that same moment, gently squeezed the trigger. The rifle slapped against her shoulder – hard. The whistle sound merged into long bubbling scream of agony. The

NCO's hands fanned the air frantically. His knees started to crumble beneath him like those of a new-born calf. Next instant he pitched face-forward into the snow and lay still.

It was the signal the Red Ravens had been waiting for. They opened fire. The first volley crashed into the line of advancing Germans. Fritzes went down everywhere, suddenly galvanized into frenetic lethal activity, bowled over, slapped against the boulders by the impact of the slugs smacking into their bodies, doubling crazily for cover. Next moment the first wild flurry of bullets began to patter against the Ravens' positions. The battle for the Chotyu-Tau Pass had commenced ...

SIX

As the echo of that first startling volley rolled and rolled dramatically down the valley, the first gentle, feathery flakes of a new snowfall began to trickle down, growing in intensity by the instant.

'Return fire—' Colonel Stuermer began, his voice snatched away by the sudden wind, which had already started whipping the snow into their bent faces and stinging tears from their blinking eyes.

Within seconds, visibility was down to a metre and they were blanketed in an impenetrable cocoon of swirling white. Colonel Stuermer ducked. A burst of automatic fire whined off the rocks to his right in a murderous ricochet. Everywhere, scarlet flame stabbed the whirling white gloom, as their attackers fired blind at the mountaineers. Stuermer flung a hasty prayer to heaven. This day God had been looking after them. Undoubtedly Stormtroop had suffered some casualties, but the sudden snowstorm was now giving them all the protection they needed.

He cupped his hands around his mouth. 'Return fire,' he yelled with all his strength; then, 'Meier and Jap – to me! Over here – quick now!'

An instant later the two NCOs emerged from the snow.

'Listen, you two,' he yelled above the howling wind, 'I want two volunteers to come with me up the track. We've got to find out the kind of opposition we're facing. Major Greul on the right can't put in an attack until he knows what he's up against.'

'And I suppose we're the two volunteers, sir?' Jap grunted.

'That's right. How did you guess?'

'I just felt it somehow, sir,' Jap replied and tugged his snow smock closer to his skinny frame.

'You'll be feeling the toe of my boot up yer arse – somehow,' Ox-Jo snarled. 'When do we start, sir?'

'Now . . . Come on.'

Bent almost double against the howling wind, which whipped the snowflakes into their crimson streaming faces like white tracer, the three men worked their way along a line of broken rock, hardly noticing the stray slugs which whined off it every now and again. In comparison with this howling crazy onslaught by Nature, man-made viciousness seemed relatively harmless.

Stuermer stumbled to a halt at the edge of the track which led upwards. They had left it early, because he had reasoned that if the pass were held, its defenders would have a fixed machine-gun covering it, firing regularly at intervals, its range already set.

The next moment his guess was proved right. There was the chatter of a heavy machine-gun. Red glowing tracer zipped through the whirling white fog. Slugs howled off the rock a couple of metres away from them. Stuermer didn't hesitate 'Come on – quick,' he commanded, and broke cover. Madly the three of them, bodies bent double, scurried across the trail and pitched into the deep snow of the other side, just as the machine-gun fired its next vicious burst.

Doggedly, the three men began to stumble up the mountainside, slipping and falling time after time on the treacherous surface of the new snow, bodies wet with sweat in spite of the biting cold, faces whipped mercilessly by the bitter flying flakes. The ascent seemed interminable. No-one spoke. The only sound was the harsh rasping of their own breath. Their sole concern was not the enemy, but the physical effort of keeping going, fighting the vicious whirling snow.

Then, as suddenly as it had commenced, the snow-storm started to peter out. Visibility began to improve. The wind dropped and the intensity of the flakes diminished. Now Colonel Stuermer, in the lead, could catch glimpses of the great swell of Elbrus with to its front the sharp twin peaks on either side of the pass. He knew that it would only be a matter of minutes before the snow storm stopped altogether and they would be completely exposed to the unknown defenders' view. He decided they could go no further. 'Hit the dirt,' he ordered.

They needed no urging. The storm had taken its toll. They were exhausted. Wearily, the two of them slumped behind the cover of the nearest boulder, while Colonel Stuermer wormed his way forward in order to get a better view of the summit. The last few feathery flakes melted on his face. Stuermer blinked a couple of times to clear them from his eyelids, then squirming round on his back in the hollow in which he found himself, he pulled out his metal shaving mirror.

Slowly, very slowly, he raised it above his head. Nothing happened. No angry burst of fire. The mirror had not been spotted. For a moment he could see nothing. The steel was misted from the heat of his body. But only for an instant; the chill mountain air soon cleared the grey film and he could see the top of the pass. Gingerly he turned the mirror, grateful that there was no sun to betray the shining surface, and covered the heights. Soon a dark figure came into view – and another. He held the mirror still and surveyed them. Then he nearly dropped the mirror. The bigger of the two figures had thrown back its snow hood to reveal a full head of blonde curls. The defenders of the Chotyu-Tau Pass were women!

'Women or no women, Greul,' Stuermer said firmly 'they've got a beautiful position up there!' He drew a line in the snow with his knife. 'They're covering it – here and here, with a fixed line machine-gun – here. Then,' he paused and let the ragged burst of firing from the other Edelweiss's position die away, telling himself that they were carrying out his order to keep the defenders occupied during the night, 'they've got another couple of machine-guns over to their right – here and here.'

Greul nodded sombrely and flicked off the torch with which he had illuminated the little sketch in the snow. At first he had sniffed contemptuously when Stuermer had explained that the pass was defended by women. He had urged an all-out attack from the right, where his own force, still unspotted by the Russian women, was located. But the second snow blizzard, and Colonel Stuermer's description of the enemy position, had now made him more cautious. 'What do you suggest then, sir?'

'We've no chance at all of taking the pass by direct assault, Greul,' Stuermer answered, selecting his words with care. 'A flank attack by your people might well have some initial surprise success. But remember the terrain and the depth of the snow up there. They would have time enough to recover and exposed like they would be, your men would be sitting ducks.'

'Not at night,' Greul objected.

'Agreed. But they would still take heavy casualties and I cannot afford any more serious losses. In the last seventy-two hours we have suffered over twenty-five casualties and God knows what else faces us once we have cleared the pass. I need all the men I can find.'

'I understand, sir. But what are we going to do?'

'This.' Swiftly Stuermer explained the plan that had been forming in his mind over the last hour, as he had wrestled with the problem of clearing the pass without any further losses.

For a moment Greul said nothing when Stuermer was finished. There was no sound save the howl of the night wind and the odd crack of riflefire from the other Stormtroop position. Then he said slowly and thoughtfully, 'It's going to be hell, sir.'

'Yes, hell – and then some,' Colonel Stuermer was forced to agree.

SEVEN

Sergeant Lermintov sipped her black tea, liberally laced with vodka, and stared down the mountainside. It was a beautiful dawn. The sky above was a hard, glittering blue and the slope below was an eye-blinking, perfect white. But the cropped-haired Sergeant had no eyes for the beauty of the summer morning; her gaze was fixed on the dark motionless shapes, capped here and there by a mound of snow, which were the Fritz dead, with, beyond, the little occasional spurts of scarlet that indicated the enemy was still firing back but was not making any attempt to out-flank their position.

'Well, Comrade Sergeant?' petite, baby-faced Ilona Serova, who had brought her the canteen of tea, asked, as they crouched together in the firing pit next to the machine-gun.

'I was just thinking, my sweet Ilona,' the Sergeant growled in that gruff masculine bass she had begun to affect as soon as she had donned the earth-coloured uniform of the Alpine Corps in '41 and had been able at last to display her true sexual inclinations, 'that we have the Fritzes by their short and curlies.'

The girl giggled. 'The expressions you use, Comrade Sergeant!'

'I could use others. But no matter,' Sergeant Lermintov said, obviously very pleased with herself, and finished her tea with a flourish. 'All right, Ilona Serova, I'm off back up to the caves. And keep those pretty eyes of yours peeled – or some hairy Fritz'll be up your knickers before you know it.'

Again the girl giggled, while Sergeant Lermintov eased her enormous bulk through the snow towards the cave from whence she would radio the captain in Elbrus House that all was quiet on the Chotyu-Tau Pass front.

It had been a murderous climb. The four of them – Stuermer, Greul, Ox-Jo and Jap – had started out in yet another blizzard, the heavy wet snow melting and trickling through

107

every gap in their clothing and sticking to their boots in huge clumps so that they had been thoroughly miserable, their leg muscles burning with pain, by the time they had arrived at the bottom of the ascent.

By then it had stopped snowing. That had been a blessing. The only one, for as Stuermer had predicted to Greul, the ascent was 'hell – and then some'. He had led himself. Reaching up, he had found a hold in the darkness and heaved. The ascent had commenced. For a while everything had gone well. He knew it was madness to climb an unknown mountain in the middle of the night. But somehow the challenge of the unknown had brought to full flower his skill, revealing to him capabilities and knowledge that he thought he had lost long before in his youth. Then they had run into shale, covered by wet snow. A sixty-five minute miserable slog had commenced, agonizing step-by-step up the treacherous slippery surface, with all four of them falling every few minutes, slithering down into the darkness, muffling their curses and the noise as best they could, their bodies bruised and slashed by the sharp edges of the shale.

At five Stuermer had been forced to order a rest. Gratefully Ox-Jo eased the mortar tube off his bruised shoulders and lay full length in the snow, as if he were lying on a down quilt. Within minutes he was snoring, while the other three had huddled there on the ledge in miserable shivering silence.

At five-thirty, knowing that they could rest no longer, Stuermer had ordered them to begin climbing again. This time Greul took the lead, while he brought up the rear, carrying the mortar tube across his back now.

Now the going had been even worse. They had run into a *couloir*, a deep V-shaped fissure in the mountain side, its rocky walls almost sheer, with here and there the face choked with high mounds of frozen snow, shaped by the bitter wind into fantastic shapes.

It had been a murderous, back-breaking business to conquer the *couloir*. Greul had displayed all that talent which had made him Germany's best young climber before the war, hammering in spike after spike, leading them ever higher with seemingly tireless ease. But even his talent failed him when they came to the snow mounds. The snow crust had been too thin to bear their weight so that at every step they had broken through and sunk in – sometimes up to their waists. Repeatedly they had been forced to stop and use their axes to remove the huge balls of snow that had collected under their boots and made their every movement as ponderous as a deep-sea diver's.

By six, just as the first ugly white of the false dawn had begun to flush the sky, they had overcome the *couloir*. But they had still not completed that terrible ascent. Before them lay perhaps some two hundred metres of almost sheer rock. Now Stuermer had taken the lead again, handing the mortar tube back to Ox-Jo, while Greul, carrying the bombs strapped to his soaked back, brought up the rear. After a couple of abortive attempts, Stuermer found the crack he sought. It ran in a slanting fashion across the rock, but it did go upwards. Time was running out and Stuermer knew he could not afford to look for anything better. It would have to do.

What had followed had been a nightmare, a brutal, lung-rasping nightmare, with the wind and the occasional bitter flurry of snow, tearing at their faces and trying to rip them from the surface of the rock face to which they clung like pathetic human flies, dwarfed by the might of that majestic mountain panorama.

It had been an interminable burning agony of hanging on with muscles which were afire, and toes and fingertips which felt as they might fall off at any moment, taking suicidal risks that no mountaineer in his right mind should ever take, hammering in spike after spike, repeating the same double-hitch, and crawling centimetre by centimetre up the sheer face to the ledge which seemed to be a million kilometres away.

One hour later, with the first rays of the sun casting a blood-red hue over his sweat-lathered face. Colonel Stuermer slid over the edge of the cliff, collapsing there in a spent shapeless heap, his body racked with pain, his breath coming in great hectic rasping gasps, unable to hear, see, think for what seemed an age.

Then, like an old, old man, he raised himself, forcing his body to forget the murderous burning pains, aware again of the steel ring of climbing boots against rock and spike, telling himself that his comrades had not yet completed that terrible climb and that he must help them.

Using his last reserves of strength, he plucked the mortar tube from its straps on Meier's broad back and heaved it over the top. Next moment he had helped Meier himself over the top, where he flopped face forward into the snow, gasping with relief. The mortar shell-box on Greul's back followed and even the arrogant National Socialist major did not disdain a helping hand this time. Jap brought up the rear and on this occasion the descendant of generations of Himalayan porters and Bavarian cowherds was as exhausted as the rest of them: the ascent had taken full toll of the wiry yellow half-breed's normally indefatigable staying-power. The little team was beat to the world.

It was now an hour after dawn. Stuermer had forced them all to eat a little of their hard dried meat, washed down with a mouthful of melted snow. They had protested that they weren't hungry, just exhausted. But he had insisted, knowing that they needed new energy for the task ahead. Then, like a careful mother rewarding her brood for some particularly good deed, he had solemnly handed each one of them a piece of dextrose sugar. The sweet tablets, he knew, would flood swift energy into their bloodstreams.

Slowly they began to rouse themselves from their lethargy, while Stuermer, lying full length in the snow, surveyed the women's positions below.

Ox-Jo crawled to him, dragging the mortar tube. 'Heaven, arse and twine, sir!' he cursed in awe when he saw the Russians. 'Women – a good dozen of them – in the middle of nowhere and us poor troopers without any of that good stuff for days on end. What a waste of talent!'

Stuermer sniffed. 'You might be right. There could well be some better use for their charms. But I'm afraid at this particular moment, those Russian women simply spell trouble for Stormtroop Edelweiss.'

Ox-Jo grinned hugely. 'Let Mrs Meier's little boy get down there among them, sir, and I'd soon show you how to deal with them. Club them over the head with a certain blunt instrument.'

Stuermer smiled faintly and then his smile vanished as the full impact hit him of what they must do next. There were no two ways about it: the women would have to be eradicated if the Stormtroop were to pass to Elbrus. 'All right, Meier,' he snapped, 'start setting up the tube.' He squirmed round and commanded, 'Jap, get that base plate over here.'

Swiftly the four men began setting up the 47mm mortar, Jap laying the base plate, while Ox-Jo screwed in the tube. At their side, Major Greul shucked the bulbous deadly winged bombs out of their cardboard cases and laid them next to the mortar in the snow. For his part, Colonel Stuermer estimated the distance and made the necessary adjustment to the range metre and the angle. Like the trained, veteran team they were, the four of them were ready to fire within a matter of brief minutes. Stuermer nodded to Greul. 'You take over the firing Greul. You're our best shot. Immediately I give the word, fire – don't hesitate!' He nodded to Ox-Jo, 'You can load, and remember to keep them coming, once the firing commences.'

'Right, sir.'

'Jap, you come with me.'

Quickly the two men squirmed through the deep snow until they were directly overlooking the women's positions some one hundred and fifty metres below.

'All right, Jap, we've got to smoke them out of those holes. And we've got exactly six bombs to do it with. So we can't afford to make mistakes. We've got to panic them into running into the open. Then it will be our job to—' He left the rest of the sentence unsaid.

Jap nodded. 'I understand, sir.'

'On no account must they be allowed to bury themselves into those holes of theirs. Then we'll never get them out. We'll be marking time in front of this damned pass until Doomsday. All right, here we go!'

The red flare hissed into the hard blue sky with startling suddenness. Everywhere the Red Ravens turned in their holes to stare at it, their handsome faces bathed a blood-red hue, their abruptly damp hands clutching their weapons in frightened tension.

'What the dev—'

The words died on Sergeant Lermintov's abruptly dry lips. There was an obscene thick belch, followed an instant later by the stomach-churning howl of a mortar firing. She caught a glimpse of the little black bomb hurtling slowly into the sky and then it had gone, and she knew from her experience on the Moscow Front the previous winter that the bomb was swooping down on their positions faster than the eye could see.

'The pricks have got behind us!' she yelled. '*Down, everywhere!*'

Her curses were drowned by the earth-shaking explosion of the mortar bomb. The ground came up and slapped her hard in the mouth. Her nostrils flooded with the acrid choking stink of cordite. Shaking her head violently to rid it of the ringing, she blinked her eyes several times and stared about her. The shell had scored a direct hit on Ilona Serova's foxhole. Now it was a smoking mass of fresh brown soil. There was no sign of the girl. Then Sergeant Lermintov saw it, and caught her scream just in time. The thing rolling slowly across the plateau which looked like an abandoned football was Ilona Serova's head!

But Sergeant Lermintov had no time to indulge herself in shocked emotionalism. Above them on the height which overlooked the pass and which she had thought was unscaleable, the mortar spewed scarlet flame again. Another bomb sped into the sky until it had achieved the necessary height before beginning to fall upon the panic-stricken women at a tremendous speed, trailing its obscene frightening howl behind it. She ducked her head. In that same instant, the bomb exploded right in the middle of the plateau. Fist-sized, gleaming-silver fragments howled everywhere alarmingly. She felt something strike her helmet a glancing blow. Red and white stars exploded in front of her eyes. For an instant she thought she was going to faint. By a sheer effort of will, she fought off the dark wave of unconsciousness that threatened to swamp her. Instead she raised her machine pistol and fired a wild burst at the height, watching with a feeling of helplessness the slugs striking the snow impotently, below where the German mortar was located. Their weapons simply did not have the range. And then the whole plateau was engulfed in a hot, choking, earth-shaking, furious barrage and the Krupp steel was ripping, gouging, tearing, slicing their soft female bodies, leaving their foxholes a smoking horror of mangled, limbless bodies, swimming purposely in their own thick hot red gore; and the survivors were up streaming wildly across the red snow, throwing away their weapons in their mindless panic, blind and deaf to her warnings, running directly into the German machine-gun fire.

Far above, Stuermer shook his head, his lean face white with shock at the way the women had run straight into their fire, leaving their young bodies sprawled across the snow-covered plateau like abandoned bundles of rags. Slowly he let his smoking machine pistol sink, his shoulders slumped with weary despair. Why had the women to die? But he knew there was no answer to that overwhelming question. He might as well have asked why there should be war. 'Cease fire, Jap,' he commanded, his voice filled with an almost unbearable weariness. 'Cease firing – the pass is ours!'

Summoning up the last of his strength, trying not to see the still black shapes below, he raised his flare pistol and fired the green Verey light, which signalled their victory to the men waiting below. The battle for the Chotya-Tau Pass was over ...

Section Four

THE RED RAVENS

ONE

Colonel Stuermer picked up a handful of the loose snow, which covered the edge of the glacier and let it melt in his parched mouth. He fought off the temptation to swallow it – he knew that would result in diarrhoea. Instead, his burning thirst quenched a little, he spat out the snow and stared wearily at the task that now confronted his tired mountaineers, who were slumped in the snow all around him.

All that morning they had been climbing through a raging blizzard. Heavy wet snow had swirled around them in a thick blanket, sifting down inside their tunics and mountain boots, blocking their eyes and mouths, turning their hands into leaden lumps of ice which could hardly feel their alpenstocks. Now the blizzard had ceased, but he knew as he stared at the glacier which barred any further progress that the going was bound to continue to be just as difficult and back-breaking.

The glacier stretched as far as the eye could see, gleaming a dull menacing grey in spite of the lack of sun. He sucked his teeth, which ached constantly at this height, and told himself that there were sure to be crevasses, some of them probably covered over with a light, treacherous roof of snow; and with visibility the way it was, it would be difficult to pick out the usual telltale warning signs that indicated the presence of a crevasse. The prospect before him and Stormtroop Edelweiss was definitely uninviting, but there was no other way up Mount Elbrus. It had to be taken or they would have to turn back.

'All right,' he croaked through cracked, parched lips, wishing as he spoke that he could simply lie down in the soft wet snow and go to sleep and forget his raging headache and his aching teeth, 'rope up. We're going on.'

Slowly, with fingers that felt like clumsy sausages, his weary mountaineers began to comply with his order, while Stuermer gave his final instructions to Major Greul who would follow him as number two onto the glacier. 'I know the old rule –

never go two on a glacier, Greul, but there is no other way to do it. We'll keep a distance of – say – ten metres between each man. That way if anyone goes into a crevasse, he won't drag his neighbour in with him.'

Greul nodded his understanding.

'We'll also ensure that there is enough spare rope to use for rescue purposes, in case an accident happens.'

'I suggest about twenty metres!'

'Agreed.'

The men were ready now, but Stuermer had one final instruction for them. 'Use your Prusik slings,' he commanded.

Obediently, the men attached the device to the rope which linked them together, one sling near the body, its loose end passed through the waist loop and tucked into the pocket of their tunics, the other thrust along the rope until its free end was within easy reaching distance.

'Good,' Stuermer praised when they were finished. 'All right, you men know the drill. Watch the man in front of you all the time – don't worry about the surface of the glacier. I'll guide you over that. Don't let your section of the rope go slack, and have your axe ready for a quick belay in case of trouble.' 'He took a deep breath, feeling the icy air slice into his strained lungs painfully. *'Follow me!'*

Now Colonel Stuermer was no longer cold. His body dripped, indeed, with sweat: the sweat of tension and fear. Now they were well onto the glacier, strung out right across its dull-gleaming surface, with the colonel in the lead, probing with the tip of his axe before he took a step forward, wondering, when the tip went in deeper than it should, whether he dared risk it.

At regular intervals, Stuermer stopped to give his exhausted men a breather and at the same time to check for the tell-tale crevasse shadows. So far Edelweiss had been lucky. They had managed to avoid crevasses and there had not been a single serious fall on the treacherous surface of the glacier. But visibility was bad and he knew he had to hurry his men if they didn't want to be caught still out on the glacier by the advent of darkness. That would be fatal.

He pushed on, working his way round the hummocks of ice, circumventing the deep ice fissures, taking his life into his hands to spring across the smaller ones and hoping that the thin film of snow on the far side would bear his weight, the knowledge that it was getting progressively darker all the time constantly at the back of his mind.

It was about four that afternoon when it happened. They had just surmounted the highest point of the glacier and were beginning the descent which would place them directly below Elbrus House, which lay somewhere in the gloom a thousand metres above them. Suddenly, completely without warning, the ground gave way beneath his feet. His axe flew out of his startled hand and he was falling at an alarming rate in a great flurry of snow. A jerk, which knocked the breath out of him. The rope around his waist held. But he was still falling. For a moment he panicked. If he didn't stop soon, that would be that. A second jerk. The rope cut painfully into his stomach. He gasped with both pain and fear. *Would it hold?* The question flashed through his mind. But the stout rope held, and abruptly he was swinging there wildly, gasping for breath, his startled eyes trying to see in the glowing semi-darkness of the deep crevasse into which he had fallen.

He calmed himself and started to work swiftly. He knew that the pressure of the rope cutting into his waist would render him unconscious in a few minutes if he didn't relieve it at once. With fingers that were shaking wildly, he fought the Prusik sling, trying to lever it down his body so that he could get one foot in it, feeling the black waves of unconsciousness streaming back and forth, threatening to swamp him at any moment.

Then he had done it and the pressure was relieved from his chest; his weight supported now by the sling around his right foot, the black waves banished. He took a deep breath and hoping that every one above was obeying the standing order in such circumstances not to unrope and try to help him, he surveyed his surroundings. He had fallen into a deep crevasse – how deep he could not tell in the dim glow. But he could make out that the hole into which he had slipped was of the worse kind : broad at the bottom and narrow at the top. It would be a beast to get out of, when the ice walls on either side were far beyond his reach.

Stuermer knew he must get started. The hole was freezingly cold. If he didn't move soon, his limbs would grow numb and refuse to function. He breathed out hard and commenced the back-breaking, interminably slow ascent up a makeshift lad-der of slings. First the weight off one foot, followed by thrust-ing the Prusik sling higher up the rope which held him, foot back in the sling and jamming the knot. Now the same proce-dure with the other foot. Higher and higher, the muscles of his arms and legs afire in an agony of pressure, feeling the strength ebb from his lean, trained body, as if someone had opened a tap and let it drain out.

The climb seemed to take an eternity : a nightmarish eter-nity, an endless numbing time of racked, tortured muscles, with the deadly cold gripping at him with icy fingers, attempt-ing to pluck him into that lethargy of inaction which would be death itself.

With all his mental strength, the source of that power which had made him Germany's finest climber, he forced himself to drain all thought and all emotion out of his tortured body and concentrate solely and exclusively on each new move, turning himself into a climbing machine.

Foot by foot, centimetre by centimetre, he raised himself up the crevasse, the only sound the harsh rasp of his own breath and the metallic scrape of his boots on the sling. Now it was getting lighter. He was close to the exit. He could hear voices, faint and far away, yet somehow anxious. He fought on. His comrades had not abandoned him.

Suddenly his head bumped into something. He looked up, startled. The rope which was holding him had bitten deep into the overhanging snow lip of the crevasse's exit! Now the mound of snow barred his way. He would have to clear it in order to get out. But he had lost his axe. He cursed bitterly and for the first time felt like giving in. Bitter tears of self-pity trickled down his ashen, frozen face. How could he get through that frozen mass?

Then, miraculously, the ice began to give. At first it was only slivers which fell onto his upturned pathetic face. But soon the slivers became chunks and he ducked his head into his shoulders in order not to be hurt by the rain of ice.

The voices became clearer. He recognized one of them. It was Jap's. 'Get the h—' he attempted to warn the little corporal, but he didn't have the strength to complete his warning. Instead he hung there and let it happen.

A few moments later, Jap had broken through and Stuermer was staring up in numb astonishment at the half-breed's face. For a moment he couldn't understand what was wrong with him; then Jap gasped, 'Hurry up, sir. Here's the rope! That big Bavarian barnshitter is holding me by the feet and I don't know how much longer he can hang on to me.'

Gratefully Stuermer accepted the rope and looped it round his waist the best he could. Now two ropes held him just under the lip of the crevasse. Jap disappeared. Ox-Jo's voice commanded, 'All right, you bunch of wettails – *pull*!'

Next instant Colonel Stuermer, more dead than alive, felt himself being tugged free from the lethal grasp of the crevasse.

Now it was night, and the utterly weary men, who had managed to cross the glacier just before complete darkness had descended upon them, were squatting in their tents, cooking their evening meal – an appalling mess of oatmeal, cocoa-powder and strawberry jam, generously laced with condensed milk – over the flickering spluttering tommy cookers.

Stuermer had already eaten, thanks to a concerned Ox-Jo, had just finished bathing and bandaging Greul's hands, which had been cruelly cut when he had been forced to take Stuermer's full weight at the crevasse, and was now smoking the finest pipe he had ever enjoyed in his whole life.

'I thought I was going to have to look at the potatoes from underneath that time, Greul,' he confessed, breathing out a stream of blue smoke pleasurably. 'That crevasse was a bitch.'

For once the keep-fit fanatic, who abhorred all stimulants, did not object to his C.O.'s smoking in the close confines of the two-man tent. 'Yessir, it was definitely dicey.' He winced.

'Does it hurt, Greul?' Stuermer said concerned. 'You should have taken the aspirin.'

Greul shook his head firmly. 'The new German must learn to accept and bear pain,' he announced, trotting out one of those National Socialist clichés which Stuermer detested.

For once, Stuermer did not allude to it. Instead, he said, 'Why don't you get into your sack, Greul and try to get some rest? It'll ease the pain. I'll take first duty. I've recovered now.' He smiled at the other man, whose face was white with pain, his liquid eyes clearly revealing that his hands were burning like hell. 'Off you go, that's an order now.'

Without protest, Greul crept into the bag and turned his suffering face to the wall, while Stuermer dressed, took one last long suck at his pipe before putting it out, and crawled into the star-studded, icy velvet darkness of the mountain night.

From the tents grouped behind the overhang, there came the sporadic, hushed talk of weary men, preparing to turn in for the day. For a moment or two, Stuermer listened, reassured to hear that his men were not complaining about their lot, cut off in the middle of enemy territory, attempting to scale an unknown mountain at the idle whim of the 'Greatest Captain of All Time', as the National Socialist hierarchy called their Führer without the slightest shame. Instead their talk was that of soldiers everywhere: women, food, duty – and women again. He smiled to himself in the glowing darkness. As long as his mountaineers stuck to 'subject number one', as they called women, there would be nothing to fear.

Slowly he plodded through the deep snow, checking the sentries posted all around the little camp. The men were alert in spite of the murderous gruelling day on the glacier and he spent a few minutes with each man, exchanging the usual meaningless conversation that was customary between a C.O. and an ordinary soldier, yet knowing those few minutes meant something to the soldier; it cemented the bond between superior and subordinate.

Now he knew he could have returned to the tent and slept; everything was under control. But the activity and alarms of the day had left him tired in body, yet alert in mind. In spite of his physical weariness, he pulled himself up and climbed over the top of the ledge which hid their camp.

The snow glittered like diamonds in the bright moonlight, and visibility was excellent. Standing there alone, no sound disturbing the silence of the night save the faint hiss of the wind moving over the surface of the snow, he stared at the heights above him. Again he felt that sense of impotence and unimportance when confronted by the enormous majesty of the high mountains, and the immense velvet-silver sweep of the glowing night sky. How insignificance he – Man – was in the face of Nature! What did human existence, with its petty, squalid, minute progress, signify in such a world? A man's whole life was nothing but a pin-scratch on the endless wall of history.

Standing there, with the wind brushing the snow against his immobile body, like a supplicant praying in front of some great altar, Colonel Stuermer wished fervently that the war would be over and he could do the only thing he still wanted to achieve in this life: the ascent of that remote 'German Mountain'[1] that had been his dream ever since he had begun climbing.

But Colonel Stuermer's dream was an idle one. Even as he stared upwards, dreaming a dream that was manifestly impossible, a long boatlike shape emerged momentarily out of the sparkling gloom. It was Elbrus House, and for one instant before it sailed silently back into the night again, Colonel Stuermer saw that lights blazed from its porthole-like windows. His heart sank. Elbrus House was occupied, and that could mean only one thing: fresh bloodshed.

[1] See *Stormtroop I* for further details.

TWO

'*Oh, my God*—' Roswitha Mikhailovna caught herself just in time. She must not frighten her Red Ravens. 'Quick,' she ordered, 'bring her inside!'

A half-dozen hands hurried to help the grievously injured woman. Gently they escorted Sergeant Lermintov to the steel table in the centre of the main hall, blood trailing across the hall from her wounded leg, and laid her there.

Roswitha drew her knife. Swiftly and expertly she slit the blood-stained clothing from the sergeant's gross body, leaving her naked, her terrible wounds revealed to their frightened eyes.

Lydia bent over the sergeant and then drew away, her pretty face wrinkled in immediate disgust.

'What is it?' Roswitha asked, dropping the soaked bloody rags on the floor and looking at the gaping wounds in the sergeant's right leg and right breast, which had been almost shot away.

'Take a smell at that, Comrade Captain,' Lydia answered thickly, holding her hand in front of her mouth, as if she might be sick at any moment.

Roswitha bent and smelled the unconscious sergeant's body. The stench was vile. Bile rose in her throat and she pulled her head away hastily. 'Gas gangrene,' she announced. 'God knows how the poor one managed it this far!'

'What can we do?' Lydia asked.

'Nothing,' Roswitha said with more conviction than she felt. She knew she must keep her head, set an example. The Red Ravens might well be as courageous as any man, yet they were still women with all their female revulsions at physical disfigurement. The sight of the gross sergeant's terribly hurt body might well panic them.

Sergeant Lermintov's eyes flickered, opened, closed and then opened again. It seemed to take her an age to recognize Roswitha Mikhailovna. 'Drink . . . drink,' she croaked. . . . 'Drink, please.'

Roswitha clicked her fingers. One of the Red Ravens thrust a bottle of vodka into her hand. Supporting the sergeant's neck, she raised her and held the bottle to her mouth.

Lermintov gulped greedily at the bottle, gagging, spluttering, coughing as the fiery spirit trickled down her parched throat. 'Good . . . good,' she gasped.

Gently, but firmly, Roswitha pulled the bottle away from her lips.

'Comrade Lermintov,' she said speaking very slowly and clearly, 'what happened?'

'They—'

'The Fritzes?' Roswitha interjected.

'Yes, the Fritzes. We thought we had them pinned down. Our position was so good. I'd—'

'Tell me what happened, please, comrade.' On a sudden impulse she smoothed the sergeant's cropped dark hair out of her bleeding mask of a face.

'They caught us . . . off guard . . . Up on the height.' Sergeant Lermintov groaned from deep down in her tortured throat. The moan set Roswitha's teeth on edge. At her side she felt Lydia's hand creep into her own, perhaps with fear. She pressed it hard to reassure the girl – and herself. 'Go on, comrade,' she urged, trying to keep her voice steady.

'They wiped out the girls . . . We didn't have a chance . . . They panicked . . . ran right into the Fritz fire.'

'And you?'

'I stuck it out in my hole, although I was wounded . . . Then when . . . when they stopped firing, I . . . I ran away.' She looked up at Roswitha with eyes that were liquid with pain. 'Did I do wrong, Comrade Captain?' she asked plaintively.

'Of course not, sergeant,' she answered. 'How brave you were to climb up here with your wounds. Comrade Stalin will learn of this.'

'Thank you,' the grievously wounded woman whispered. 'I tried all my life to be like a man . . .'

'And where are they now?' Roswitha said when the other woman's words had trailed into nothing.

'Down . . . down,' Sergeant Lermintov tried to raise herself, but she had no strength left. 'Down . . .' Suddenly her frozen, bloody face lolled to one side, forlorn and lifeless like that of a broken doll.

Swiftly Roswitha held the face of her wristwatch close to the sergeant's gaping mouth. The glass remained clear. She wasn't breathing any more. She felt Lydia's hand gripping her own more tightly with fear. 'Give me a blanket,' she said, forcing herself to keep her voice calm and unemotional. 'Sergeant Lermintov is dead. She died for her Motherland.' Slowly and respectfully she spread the army blanket across the gross Lesbian body, while Lydia sobbed softly at her side.

'Comrades,' Roswitha said sombrely, staring around at their faces, and telling herself that although they had recovered from the shock of the sergeant's death, they were still nervous and a little apprehensive, 'it is clear that the enemy is heading this way. It is clear, too, that the Fritzes are a determined, experienced group of mountaineers. Only skilled climbers could have managed to surmount that peak and come up behind the pass. So, comrades, we have a problem on our hands.'

'What do you mean, Comrade Captain?' Lydia asked and Roswitha could see that the nervous tic at the side of her pretty face had still not vanished. Hastily she fought back the impulse to rush across and comfort her.

'This. This afternoon the *Stavka* signalled that the Army is beginning to move troops into the area beyond the Elbrus. Finally the Comrade Generals have taken our warning about the enemy intentions seriously. If those Fritzes manage to penetrate our line and cross the mountains, then they will not only have pioneered a way for more Fritzes to follow, they will also have discovered our new dispositions. They will know that we have weakened the Black Sea front in order to cover the mountains. That might mean their generals may decide to attack through our weakened Black Sea front after all.' She licked her dry lips. 'Don't you see, my Red Ravens, if we don't stop the Fritzes here, they could be in a position to roll up our whole front and thrust deep into the Caucasus?'

'But what can we do, Comrade Captain?' Lydia asked. 'There are only a few of us – and they are real soldiers, trained and . . .' the words trailed away into nothing as she saw the look on Roswitha's face.

'That was unworthy of you, Lydia, unworthy of the Red Ravens, unworthy of us as women. Aren't we trained soldiers, too? Aren't we trained mountaineers?' Roswitha Mikhailovna wagged her finger at the pale-faced pretty girl in the same manner she had seen Comrade Stalin himself use often enough. 'No one wanted this terrible war, but in a way it is a blessing for us women. Now we can show that we are every bit as good as our male comrades. We are no longer the stupid housewife of old, her only concern kitchen, cooking and children. We are the new generation of Soviet women. But we must be prepared to take the same risks and the same sacrifices as our male comrades in the Red Army.' Her voice rose. 'Comrades, if necessary, we must be prepared – *to die!*'

She allowed the terrible words to sink in, staring around at their young faces with eyes that were both hard and resolute, yet filled with a barely controlled passion, and telling herself that her Red Ravens would not let her down; they had conquered their initial fears. They would fight.

'And now, comrades, the time for talk is over. Now action counts. The Fritzes will be here by the morning, and we have a lot to do this night. *To work . . .*'

THREE

Like a gigantic metallic Pullman car, Elbrus House slid into view through the thick, milky white dawn fog. Colonel Stuermer, at the head of the column of mountaineers, held up his hand for them to stop. 'Major Greul,' he commanded, 'to me, please.'

His *Schmeisser* at the ready, Greul doubled through the snow to his waiting C.O. 'Sir?'

'Come on, we'll do a personal recce, Greul,' Stuermer answered and set off at once. This time he knew he could not afford to waste a second, if his plan were to succeed. Steadily and in silence the two of them plodded up the mountain, their footsteps crunching over the snow, deadened by the heavy wet fog. Finally Colonel Stuermer said, 'I think we're far enough, Greul. We don't want to alarm them too early, eh?'

'No, Colonel.'

Together the two officers raised their binoculars and surveyed the House. Stuermer, for one, didn't like what he saw. The long low building – it was perhaps three storeys high – was built of some heavy grey stone, covered by duraluminum, probably as protection against the mountain storms which raged almost constantly at that height in winter. On its flat roof, aerials whipped back and forth in the wind, and confirmed Intelligence's guess that Elbrus House had been used as a weather station before the war. But is wasn't only the strange house's defensive features to which Stuermer objected: it was the rape of nature that had been carried out so high in the mountains. On the backs of hundreds of men and animals, the material to build Elbrus House had been borne up the mountain – there was even a great pile of coke outside, obviously for the place's heating system. For him, Elbrus House signified the impertinence of Man in his persistent attempt to force Nature to her knees.

'A difficult place to tackle,' Greul cut into his thoughts.

'Yes, a handful of determined men could hold that place against a whole battalion,' Stuermer agreed, returning to the immediate problem. 'And by the look of that roof, the defenders might well be able to summon help or supplies by air. They could hold out there for ever and a day.'

'Agreed, Colonel.'

'And that's why we are not going to attempt to take it, Greul,' Stuermer said firmly, folding away his binoculars and looking squarely at the other officer.

'What did you say, sir?'

'You heard me, Greul. We are not going to attempt to attack it.'

'But how can we move on to the peak, sir?' Greul protested. 'There is no other way—'

'There is,' Stuermer cut him short. 'I made up my mind last night. There will be no more bloodshed on Mount Elbrus. Come on, I'll explain what we're going to do on the way back.'

Roswitha came out of the shower, completely naked as was her wont. Sitting at the table of the radio room, where she had been on radio watch during the night, Lydia's eyes travelled up and down the other woman's body with undisguised interest. 'You are very beautiful, Comrade Captain,' she said, her gaze falling on the delicate triangle of blonde down, which looked to her as smooth and sleek as the wing of some exotic bird.

She drew her gaze away by an effort of will and said, her brown doe-like eyes suddenly anxious, 'Have I shocked you, Comrade Captain?'

Roswitha Mikhailovna hesitated before she answered, her body abruptly weak, as she was overcome by a sensation she had never experienced before. 'No, Lydia,' she answered, her voice strangely husky, 'I take your words as a great compliment.' With fingers that trembled slightly, she picked up the thick woollen Army combinations.

'Must you dress already, Comrade Captain?' Lydia asked, a note of pleading in her voice.

'Why not?' she answered, pausing, knowing as she did that she was treading on dangerous ground.

'Perhaps you know.' Lydia omitted the 'comrade captain' deliberately, lowering her gaze with mock modesty.

Roswitha stared at the girl's pretty pale doll-like face, as if she were seeing her for the very first time. Suddenly she noticed that Lydia's hair was hanging loose, forming a soft frame to her face. 'No, I don't know, Lydia.'

Lydia rose and came close to her. *'You must!'* She reached out a hand, as if to touch Roswitha's naked body, then thought better of it.

'We must not indulge in emotionalism,' Roswitha answered, feeling her heart racing in a manner that she had never experienced with a man before.

'Why not?'

'The war,' Roswitha stammered. 'Our mission . . . our duty to our Soviet Motherland . . .'

'We have a duty to ourselves too, Roswitha,' the girl said softly, persuasively, perhaps already guessing the strange turmoil in Roswitha's brain. 'It needs no more courage than the first plunge of the year into a cold-water swimming pool. Convention is easily overcome. And who would know? They are all asleep . . . Why not, dear Roswitha?'

'Because.'

'Because what?'

'Because . . .' Roswitha Mikhailovna shuddered violently, as the other girl laid her cool hand on her right breast. She felt the nipple grow erect and the instant trembling of her knees, as if she might crumple and faint to the ground at any moment.

'You know,' Lydia said softly, insidiously, 'you must have known that it would end like—'

'*Comrade Captain!*' a frightened, urgent voice called from outside. Lydia withdrew her hand, as if she had been stung.

Roswitha thrust the combination to the front of her naked body. 'What is it?'

The sentry flung open the door of the radio room, her pale face flushed hectically at the cheeks, her bosom heaving with the effort of doubling down from her post on the roof. 'Comrade Captain,' she gasped. 'I've just seen them through the fog.'

'Seen who?' Captain Mikhailovna snapped, businesslike and in complete control of herself again.

'The Fritzes . . . they've arrived! They're taking up positions all around the house . . .'

The fog was still thick, but through the binoculars she could see them well enough. They were mountain troopers all right. She recognized the typical peaked cap and its *Edelweiss* badge easily enough, and even without those two items she would have been able to identify them as trained mountaineers by the way they crossed the snowfield.

'What are they going to do?' Lydia asked, and added, 'Comrade Captain', swiftly.

'I don't know, comrade.'

Roswitha swept her binoculars from left to right and followed the Germans' progress. It didn't look as if they were preparing for a frontal attack on the House because they were extending their line on either side of the building, its points hooking round in a large, encircling half moon.

'If they're gong to attack, they are a long way off, Comrade Captain,' Lydia said, expressing her own thoughts. 'Our two machine-guns would soon made short work of them at that distance and with that amount of open ground to cover. Even I can see that.'

Roswitha nodded her agreement, her pretty face creased in a puzzled frown. Lydia was right. There were at least three hundred metres between the Fritzes' positions and the House. In order to attack, they would have to cross a stretch of terrain which offered little cover save for the odd boulder. An attack in such circumstances would be a massacre. The Fritzes would have stood a much better chance if they had attacked undercover of darkness instead of advertising their presence as they were doing now. What the devil were they up to?

Stuermer blew his whistle shrilly. The men, stumbling and slipping on the snow-covered slope, came to a halt gratefully. Stuermer cupped his hands around his mouth and yelled: 'All right, start digging in now!'

The mountaineers unslung their packs, and removing their ice-axes and entrenching tools, they commenced the back-breaking task of clearing the frozen snow to make shallow protective pits against the odd rifle bullet which was already winging its way towards the extended position.

Stuermer turned to Greul, who had been plodding through the snow behind him, his arrogant face set in a look of both depression and anger.

'Well, Greul, we come to the parting of the ways,' he announced, flipping back his glove and fumbling in his pocket.

'I don't like it, sir. Give me your permission and I'll clear that pack of Red bitches out of the House within thirty minutes.'

'You probably would, my dear Greul,' Stuermer said easily. 'But unfortunately you'd loose far too many good men doing so.'

'But even if we carry out your plan, sir,' Greul objected vehemently, as a slug threw up a wild flurry of snow only metres away, 'we will still have them at our backs, forming a potential danger.'

'Yes, but that is a calculated risk we must take,' Stuermer said, finding what he had been seeking. He placed it on the palm of his hand.

Greul glared down at the little ten-pfennig piece, which in a moment would determine whether he would add Mount Elbrus to his list of 'conquests'. 'I don't like it. I don't like it one bit, sir. I must register an official protest.'

'Duly registered, Greul!' Stuermer answered, and balanced the little coin on his thumb and forefinger. 'Ready?'

'Ready,' Greul said grumpily.

Stuermer spun the coin in the air, calling 'Head, or eagle?' 'Eagle!'

Neatly Stuermer caught the little coin and showed it to Greul. 'Head,' he announced. 'I go. You stay behind.'

'Damn—' Greul caught himself in time. He was not a man given to outbursts of emotion. A good National Socialist had to be as proud as a panzer and as hard as Krupp steel; one didn't give way to one's feelings. 'Then you go, sir?'

'Yes, and you take charge here.'

'Will you take the flag?' He indicated the crooked-cross flag that was flying from the nearest position. 'The photo of your successful ascent will go around the world. Humanity must know that National Socialism has triumphed over Nature.'

Stuermer shook his head slowly, knowing as he did so that even if he managed the ascent successfully, there would be trouble – a great deal of trouble – at what he was going to do next. 'No, not the swastika. But that.' He pointed behind him.

Greul swung round.

Sergeant-major Meier, who together with Jap, had been selected to accompany Colonel Stuermer on the ascent, if the latter won the toss, was standing there with the red and white Edelweiss flag of the Stormtroop over his shoulder. He grinned impudently at the major.

Flushed and angry, Major Greul swung round and stuck out his hand. 'Colonel, may I wish you every success. *Berg Heil!*' [1]

'Thank you, Greul. *Berg Heil!*'

Five minutes later the three of them, with Colonel Stuermer in the lead left the lines of Stormtroop Edelweiss and began the first leg of the ascent, while behind them on the roof of Elbrus House, Roswitha Mikhailovna fumed with impotent rage. Five more minutes and the tiny plodding figures disappeared into the thick milk-white fog. It was now nine o'clock, and it was one thousand and five hundred metres to the top of the western summit of Mount Elbrus.

[1] A mountaineer's greeting.

Section Five

THE FINAL ASCENT

ONE

She had no fear. She thought of nothing, but breaking through the Fritz positions. But Lydia, crouching behind her with the radio on her back, was obviously afraid. Roswitha could hear her breath coming fast and shallow, as if she had just run a race. Without turning round, she reached back and patted Lydia's hand to comfort her. 'Don't worry, Lydia. Everything is under control. I can take care of them.'

'I'm all right, Comrade Captain – thank you.'

Roswitha forgot her companion. Her eyes searched the terrain to her front, probing every dip and cranny for possible sources of danger, once she had broken through. Now the fog had begun to be burned away by the sun and here and there the snow glittered with a white crystalline glare. She knew she must act soon – before the fog had disappeared altogether; she needed its cover.

She took a deep breath and gripped her pistol more firmly. 'All right, Lydia, stick close to me. Here we go!'

The first Fritz was a stocky dark-haired youth, who was working at digging a hole in the snow with whole-hearted, exclusive concentration.

She raised the pistol and fired. The slug hit him just below the rib cage. His eyes bulged and she could hear him grunt audibly as he sat down suddenly in the snow, clutching his stomach, his knuckles white.

His mate, twenty-five metres beyond, looked up, startled. He saw the woman and grabbed for his rifle which was lying on the snow next to his rucksack. She beat him to it. Her pistol cracked again. He doubled up and fell onto his knees, as if he were praying.

The third Fritz was quick. He fired instinctively. Roswitha ducked and the slug whined off the metal side of Elbrus House. Behind her, Lydia gave a little cry of fear. The pistol bucked in Roswitha's hand. The rifle flew from the Fritz's fingers. He

137

looked down at it incredulously, as if he could not understand what it was doing there on the snow. She did not give him any time to consider the problem. Her pistol spoke again. The slug caught him in the chest. At that range the impact was so great that it knocked him clean off his feet. He hit the snow with a loud thump, and then they were springing over his writhing bloody body and running up the slope.

From behind there came the first noisy cries of alarm. Bullets started to stitch the snow at their flying heels. A slug ricocheted off the metal casing of Lydia's radio. She stumbled and would have fallen, if Roswitha hadn't caught her in time. *'Keep going . . . keep going!'* she gasped.

To the enraged mountaineers, who had been taken completely by surprise by this sudden breakout, the two women were just flying blurs against the milk-white background, and accuracy in firing uphill is difficult at the best of times. All the same, their bullets were coming unpleasantly close. Bullets were kicking up white gouts of snow all around, and Roswitha knew they would be hit if they didn't make cover soon. Then she saw it. A stretch of dead ground some twenty metres further on. 'Faster,' she urged . . . *'Faster!'*

Fear lent speed to Lydia's feet. She sped forward. She passed Roswitha, the heavy radio bouncing up and down on her back. Roswitha slipped and made a catlike recovery. Something slapped against her shoulder. It stung like the devil, but she knew instinctively the bullet hadn't penetrated the thick wadding of her tunic.

Ten metres to go. The massed fire from below started to converge upon the two fugitives. Five metres. Lydia disappeared from sight. She had made it! Roswitha hesitated no longer. Summoning up the last of her energy, she dived forward into the shelter of the dead ground, landing on her stomach, all breath being knocked out of her lungs cruelly by the impact.

Fighting for breath, her lungs emptying and filling with explosive gasps, Roswitha flashed a glance at her wrist-watch. It was ten o'clock. It had taken her exactly sixty minutes to make her decision to break out and realize it. The Fritzes had an hour start.

A little groggily she struggled to her feet and offered Lydia her hand. 'Come on, my little pigeon, on your toes. We must push on.'

Lydia could not speak; she was still fighting to recover her breath. But she got up willingly enough and slung the radio more comfortably on her thin shoulders. She looked up at the sky, swallowed hard in a final effort to control her panting, and croaked, 'We might have snow, Comrade Captain, eh?'

Roswitha flashed a glance at the sky, which was again turning an ominous lead-colour. 'Perhaps,' she agreed. 'If you still pray, Lydia, begin now. We need all the help we can get.' She thrust her pistol back into its holster with a gesture of finality. 'March, my dove, we have an appointment on the mountain . . .'

TWO

The little group of Edelweiss men were making excellent progress. The rock face was broken and offered good holds and several convenient stances so that they were able to advance quickly. Stuermer was pleased, but all the same, the rock obstructions and snow mounds made it impossible for him to prospect a direct route to the summit; they blocked the view upwards too often.

By mid-morning they had covered a good five hundred metres and were going very strong. Stuermer began to think that they would realize their aim of reaching the summit and starting on their way back to Elbrus House before it grew dark again. 'Come on, the two of you,' he yelled cheerfully, his breath fogging the air in a small grey cloud, 'we'll make climbers of you yet!'

He was to realize that his sudden euphoria was due to other causes than the sense of achievement; but that was later.

Just before one o'clock the three of them bumped into their

first serious trouble of the ascent. They ran abruptly into an almost sheer rock wall, with, as far as Stuermer could see, neither holds nor stances. 'All right,' he ordered, his spirits still strangely buoyant in spite of the disappointing prospect in front of them, 'take five. I'll have a look at it.'

Gratefully, the other two slumped down on the frozen snow and with fingers that were stiff with cold, they began to eat the hard sausage they had brought with them, chewing it with relish as if they were really enjoying the rock-hard meat. They, too, seemed unaffected by the hindrance, chatting away with unusual animation, their bright-red faces very lively, their eyes gleaming.

Stuermer studied the slope. The traverse must have been one of the least attractive he had ever seen, the rock weathered, flaking and clearly unsound in many spots. Yet the realization did not seem to worry the lean colonel. Indeed, his face was wreathed in a bright smile, as if he really enjoyed the prospect of dicing with death on such a dangerous ascent.

'Well,' he announced cheerfully to the other two, a couple of minutes later, 'it's not the best traverse I've ever seen. But I think it can be done.'

'Of course, it can be done, sir!' Meier snapped, throwing away the rest of his sausage carelessly. 'But only if we get the lead out of our tails and get on with it.' He giggled suddenly and surprisingly. Nobody seemed to notice his unusual behaviour, nor the strange unnatural gleam in his bloodshot eyes.

Stuermer took the lead. To the right the ice glittered evilly on the rock face and the wind shrieked about him, as he started the traverse, seeking with his finger tips for the slightest irregularity. Centimetre by centimetre he edged his way along, powdery snow cascading down at each step. But the fact that a foothold might give way and send him tumbling down the mountain to a certain death did not seem to worry him. Once the rock did give way and he only managed to save himself by a lightning switch of his weight to the other foot. Again he remained unaffected. He was not even annoyed by Meier's fresh outburst of giggling.

The sweat pouring from his body, soaking his uniform, he

continued across and upwards. He reached a fissure. It was wider and deeper than he had first thought. 'Come on, you lucky lads,' he called down to Jap and Meier, 'this is going to be a walk-over!' Without even waiting to check their condition, he anchored himself on a good rock knob, and started upwards.

'Three cheers for Stormtroop Edelweiss!' Meier called, and followed.

'Three farts for the Führer!' Jap yelled, equally happily, and did the same.

Stuermer climbed steadily, but his strange, good mood was beginning to vanish. His head had begun to ache, and green and yellow stars were exploding in front of his eyes. Still he seemed possessed of amazing reserves of energy. He went at the rock like a man possessed and the other two followed him with the self-same strength and zest.

Suddenly there was a sharp crack. He swung round. Meier, his face abruptly contorted with fear, hands clutching at nothing, was falling!

Instinctively the colonel braced himself, flinging his whole weight against the rock face. There was a mighty tug at his shoulders. He caught himself just in time, knowing there was worse to come. The rope ran out. His waist snap-ring held. The pressure was almost unbearable, dragging him outwards. Still he held on, his face purple with strain. And the rope had not broken!

He flashed a look below. Meier was swinging in the void, three or four metres below him, while further below Jap clung to the surface of the rock, as if his very life depended upon it.

'You all right?' Stuermer called.

Meier called back something in a strangled voice, which Stuermer could not understand, yet the fear had vanished from his face.

Stuermer acted. He knew that the other man hadn't more than minutes to live, if he didn't relax the pressure of the rope constricting him soon. Gripping the waist loop with both hands and exerting strength he never knew he possessed, he swung round and faced the rock. Swiftly he made a bight with the rope and flung it over an anchor rock. An instant later he had freed himself from the rope, leaving Meier dangling there in mid-air, his big boots blindly seeking a foothold.

Taking impossible risks, Stuermer climbed down to the helpless NCO. 'Feet – here!' he gasped. Reaching out, he grabbed the other man's feet and guided them to a hold. 'Now – up you go!' The big nailed boots scraped against the rock and stuck. A few minutes later the three of them were lying on the ledge at the top of the fissure, crimson-faced and glaring at each other, as if they were deadly enemies.

'What did you want to do that for, you little yellow shit?' Meier cried at his runing-mate, murder in his eyes.

'What did I want to do what?' the other man bawled back at him, his hand instinctively reaching for his mountain knife. 'You think I let you fall?'

'Of course you did!' Meier cried, flecks of foam at the edge of his mouth. 'You were just your usual shitting careless self. Never worry—'

Stuermer flashed a glance at the altitude meter wrapped around his right wrist. The needle flickered at four thousand, six hundred metres. Suddenly he realized what the cause of their strange euphoria had been – and this equally strange quarrel between the two NCOs. 'Stop it,' he commanded. 'Shut up, will you?'

'But the big bastard accuses me—' Jap began.

Stuermer knew there was no other way. Leaning forward, he slapped the little corporal sharply across his yellow, wrinkled face.

Jap started. 'What did you have to do that for?' he demanded.

'Don't you see?' Stuermer answered urgently. 'We're nearly five thousand metres above sea level – and without oxygen. We've all got the altitude sickness!'

'That explains it,' Meier said, shaking his head, as if he was trying to wake up from a deep sleep. 'My head's throbbing, as if it's going to burst apart at any moment – and I feel, sort of light—'

'Me, too,' Jap agreed reluctantly. 'It's like not weighing

anything, as if you were made of feathers. But I feel sick with it, too. I could puke any minute.'

'All the symptoms of altitude sickness,' Stuermer said bitterly. 'That's why we took that impossible traverse. Any sane climber wouldn't have taken a risk like that.' He shook his head slowly, hating to say what he was going to say next, but knowing he must.

'We can't go on any further this day. We've got to acclimatize to the air at this altitude. Tomorrow it'll be different. Then – God willing – we'll reach the summit.'

'But what are we going to do till then?' Meier protested, his hectic look vanishing slowly now, exhaustion beginning to take its place. 'We'll freeze our nuts off if we spend the night up here in the open.'

'I know, I know, Meier,' Stuermer snapped irritably, nausea threatening to overcome him at any moment. 'We've got to find the Pastuchova Hut. It must be around here somewhere. We'll spend the night there.' Wearily he rose to his feet. 'Come on, let's get on with it.' Wordlessly the two NCOs rose and followed him, all elation vanished now.

Mount Elbrus would not be conquered this day.

THREE

'No good . . . no good, Comrade Captain, 'Lydia stuttered, 'I . . . I can't go on!'

Roswitha removed her clogged-up snow goggles and stared down at the girl, her fingers dug into the snow to hold herself against the wind which boomed and dragged along the face of the mountain. She opened her mouth to speak and the wind blew the breath back down her throat so she thought for a moment she might suffocate. She slumped down next to an exhausted Lydia and with frozen fingers started to undo the straps of the radio still attached to her back. Wordlessly she dropped it into the snow.

'Leave it?' Lydia shrieked above the wind.

'Yes. We must find them . . . without help,' Roswitha yelled back, her hands cupped around her mouth.

She stared up at the sky, flickering from burnt ochre to umber, heavy with flying snow, and told herself that even the world's best climbers would have to take cover in such conditions; and for all she knew the Fritzes were alpine soldiers, not professional climbers. But where? Where would they find cover at this altitude?

The hut! The thought flashed through her mind. Of course, it was the only place – and the Fritzes would know about it. She stumbled to her feet and chipped off the clumps of frozen snow that clung to her boots, while Lydia lay there watching her, the tears running down her ashen face and freezing to long icicles on her cheeks. Finally she was ready. 'Come on,' she shrieked.

Lydia shook her head wearily. 'Can't . . . can't go on, Comrade . . .' the tired words trailed away to nothing.

'Of course, you can. You are a Red Raven, Lydia.' Roswitha remembered that exploratory hand that had reached out and touched her naked breast; and the harshness disappeared from her voice. She bent down and took hold of Lydia's hand as tenderly as she could with her thick-gloved hand. 'Here, I shall help you.'

'But—'

'You can, Lydia. Come on.'

Lydia moaned piteously, but she got to her feet and stood there swaying unsteadily, blinking her eyes at the glowing rushing sky. Swiftly Roswitha re-attached the rope, holding Lydia's eyes with her own. She knew it was no use telling the exhausted girl to look for holds; the only thing she could do was to imprison her comrade with her own gaze, *will* her to move on and on, dragging her weary feet behind her, as if they were some great weight. 'Here.' She gave the girl her own ice-axe; Lydia had lost hers long before. 'Support yourself on that. It will help.' On sudden impulse she leaned forward and pressed her dry, cracked lips against Lydia's frozen cheek. 'We will do it,' she whispered. 'Now march!'

Dwarfed by the mountains, with the wind howling around them, attempting to pluck them from the rock face with its mighty invisible fingers, the two women, insignificant black dots against the sea of white, plodded ever onwards, hour after hour, their bodies racked with pain, the breath rasping through their tortured lungs in harsh gasps. Pebbles and frozen snow lashed at their faces and ripped open the skin. But the wind was so powerful that the blood could not seep through. Each step became a major effort of will – reach up, struggling against that immense weight which seemed to be attached there, place the foot down and take hold with fingers that felt as if they were bales of wool. On and on, with the snow falling in great wet flakes and the wind booming around the mountains with the noise of exploding artillery shells.

Once Roswitha slipped on snow-covered shale. Desperately she grabbed for a hold and screamed hysterically with pain, as the shale ripped off her thick glove and tore out the nails of her right hand at the roots. Still she went on, her hand afire with agony.

Once a great burst of wind tore at their frail bodies as they stood on a narrow rock shelf, and they clung together like two frightened children, while the wind whipped and lashed at them, as if this time it was determined to fling them to their deaths far down below.

On and on! Step by step, lurching, shaking, stumbling, suffocated by the wind, blinded by the snow, the pebbles whining off the rocks like ricochets. And then the wind began to die down. For a long while, the two pathetic mortals struggling across the face of the great mountain did not seem to notice. Chins sunk upon their breasts, they continued as before, concentrating solely on that next step. Slowly, very slowly, it seemed to dawn on them that the wind had dropped and the fury of the flying snow had begun to let up. Roswitha raised her head with infinite weariness and lifted her goggles.

Silence fell over the mountains, hurting her ears. She stared at the dying flakes in bewilderment. What did it mean? A hush began to descend upon them, and abruptly she could think clearly again. She turned to Lydia, standing there behind her numbly like a carelessly dumped sack of potatoes, and then looked at her altitude meter. It read four thousand, six hundred metres. 'Lydia,' she cried, as the snow stopped altogether, 'we've done it.'

'Wha ... what?' the other girl croaked.

'We've reached the hut! *Pastuchova Hut*!' she cried in triumph. 'Come on!'

Her headache vanished and new strength flooded back into her legs. Dragging Lydia behind her, stumbling, falling and rising again, she covered the last ninety metres. Then she saw it. The Pastuchova Hut, almost submerged in the new snow. But the thin curl of blue smoke emerging from the chimney into the evening sky told all she needed to know. It was occupied. The Fritzes were in residence!

Meier portioned out the steaming mixture of coffee, cocoa and condensed milk, and the other two clutched the canteens with their frozen fingers gratefully, their feet extended towards the tired blue flame of the primus cooker, which was as starved of oxygen as they were. They had been forced to burrow their way through the snow into the wooden hut and it had taken them an hour of murderous labour to clear its interior. Thereafter, it had been another hour before Meier had finally managed to get the mixture to boil, and he had added a massive portion of sugar to give them new energy. Now, propped up against their stiffly frozen rucksacks, they sat there, shivering, grateful for the warmth of the mixture and the flickering primus cooker, which cast strange shadows on the gloomy white interior of the snow-covered little hut.

Stuermer took a sip of the steaming mixture and felt the canteen tear at his lips. He didn't care. The drink was all-important. He could almost feel the new energy, engendered by the sugar and milk, flood into his infinitely weary limbs. 'Now, gentlemen,' he said hoarsely, 'are you still summit-hungry?' He grinned at their tired, frozen, unshaven faces.

'*Teufel und tit!*' [1] Ox-Jo growled, almost his old self again, 'of course we are. Aren't we, ape-turd?'

[1] 'Devil and tit'.

146

'Clear as chicken-soup,' Jap agreed, raising his greedy mouth from the mixture. 'I'm ready to go up alone – *now*!'

'Get off it!' Ox-Jo said. 'Showing off like ten naked niggers!'

Stuermer smiled. The two NCOs had recovered their strength, and to all appearances at least, they had overcome their altitude sickness. His own splitting headache and nausea had vanished at last. 'Do you know,' he said, 'we're higher than Montblanc, the Emperor of the Alps, now?'

Ox-Jo rubbed a massive hand, each finger split open by the cold like a burst sausage, over his bearded jaw. 'Don't know about that, sir. I'm more interested in climbing other kinds of tits than Elbrus's twin peaks.'

Stuermer laughed happily. 'And you shall have that pleasure too, once we're down again. Undoubtedly the Greatest Captain of all Times will grant Stormtroop Edelweiss a leave in the Homeland to honour our victory.'

Jap's dark eyes glinted wickedly. 'You're not pulling my pisser, are you, sir?' he demanded.

'No, your – er – pisser is quite safe, Jap.'

The corporal looked at Meier. 'Did you hear that, Ox? Remember you owe me the price of three jumps, once we get back to civilization.'

'I'll buy you a whole private knocking-shop, once we get back to Munich,' Ox-Jo agreed grandly. 'Now sir, what's the drill tomorrow morning?'

'Well, assuming the snow continues to let up, this is what we do. We dump our rucksacks and weapons here. Everything unnecessary stays behind, except the flag.'

'Not—'

'No,' Stuermer beat Ox-Jo to it. 'We just take our own Edelweiss standard.'

Ox-Jo beamed. 'That's the stuff, sir,' he said heartily. 'That'll make some people fill their breeches when they see the photos.'

Stuermer knew who 'some people' were, but he didn't comment on it. 'I'll take the camera and you, Jap, you take the bottle with our names. We'll plant it up there under a cairn. At least there'll be some proof that we made it.'

Jap sniffed. 'As you wish, sir. But I doubt if anyone will ever care, especially the Ivans. I bet they won't want to put us in their record books as the conquerors of Mount Elbrus.'

Stuermer nodded. 'I expect you're right, Jap. All right, we'll rope up immediately. I think there'll be shale or lava stone up there too and you know how damn slippy that stuff is at the best of times – and tomorrow we'll have snow and ice to contend with as well. We'll take a zig-zag course, first to the north and then once we're in sight of the twin peaks, we'll head west to take the higher of the two. We'd better do this correctly, although there is only a difference of a hundred metres in height. I know it's a propaganda exercise, but—' He shrugged and hoped that the two NCOs could understand his concern that even now it should be an honest climb. 'Well, that's about it. Any questions?'

The two NCOs shook their heads.

'All right, we'd better turn in. It's going to be a long day tomorrow.' He zipped his sleeping bag up and turned his head to one side. The other two did the same. Within minutes they were all three snoring heavily, sunk into the blessed world of sleep, in which there was no pain, no exhaustion and no cold. At their feet the primus stove flickered blue, as the first air from outside started to enter the hut ...

FOUR

Stuermer was the first to wake. The faint stirring in the snow at the entrance must have alerted something deep down within his bone-tired, sleep-drugged body. His eyes flickered open, closed, and opened again.

A face, hard and commanding, though beautiful, was staring at him from only two metres away. 'What in three ...?' he began, startled.

148

'*Be still*!' the stranger commanded in good German. '*Don't move*!'

In the eerie blue flame of the still-burning primus stove, Stuermer could see the pistol in the stranger's gloved hand, and the glacial menace in the voice told him the newcomer was deadly serious. He froze, while the stranger, pistol held erect, crawled the rest of the way into the hut and shook the hood free to reveal a swath of matted blonde hair.

Stuermer gasped involuntarily. It was a woman! Instinctively he knew that she was one of the women they had left behind at Elbrus House. Next moment another woman had followed the first inside the hut and as the two NCOs struggled awake from a deep, clinging sleep, the first snapped, 'Hands behind your heads and back against the wall!'

Awkwardly the three men struggled out of their sleeping bags and wormed their way under the low roof to the wall.

'I know you,' Ox-Jo breathed when he saw the first woman's face clearly in the light of the primus. 'You're the—'

'Be quiet!' A grimace of hate distorted the woman's face for a moment, as she shook her head to release the thick blonde hair.

Ox-Jo fell silent. The look in the woman's eyes was enough. Roswitha turned to Colonel Stuermer, whom she guessed was the officer. 'What is your name?' she demanded, while behind her, Lydia warmed one frozen hand at a time – she, too, held a pistol – in front of the primus.

'Stuermer.'

'Rank?'

'Colonel of the Alpine Corps.' Stuermer answered, feeling the grey bitterness of defeat wash through him, a sour taste in his mouth, as he realized just how easily they had been caught when they were so close to the summit.

Roswitha looked at him curiously. 'Not *the* Stuermer,' she asked, 'of the German Mountain?'

He nodded numbly.

For an instant the hard determined look on her pretty face softened. 'I have heard of you, Stuermer. Before the war I would have been proud to have made the acquaintance of a climber such as yourself. In Moscow we all had heard of you and admired your climbs. But now—' She hesitated and her face hardened again. 'Now you are a Fritz, just like the rest.' Without turning, she rapped, 'Comrade!'

'Yes, Comrade Captain?'

'The rope – and start with the big one.'

Lydia needed no further instructions. While Roswitha kept the three Germans covered with her pistol, an unwavering look in her eyes, although her injured hand was now throbbing again painfully, Lydia crawled behind a glowering Meier and started to tie his hands together by the wrist, before finally looping the rope around his big neck so that he would strangle himself if he attempted to move his wrists overly much. 'What are you trying to do, you little slit,' Ox-Jo growled sourly, 'cut my turnip off?'

Lydia, who understood no German, shrugged and crawled on to the next man, Jap. She began to repeat the performance, before starting on Colonel Stuermer, who fought off the feeling of heart-sickening defeat, telling himself that he must concentrate solely on the present, be ready to take advantage of any moment of weakness on the part of the two women.

'Now we sleep,' Roswitha announced, apparently satisfied with her companion's work. 'First my comrade and then myself. But beware, one false move and we shall shoot.'

She said something in Russian to the other girl. Gratefully Lydia crawled into the nearest sleeping bag, sighing with undisguised pleasure as she felt its warmth. Within moments she was fast asleep, not even noticing the other sleeping bag which Roswitha draped across her body gently and lovingly.

'I'd rather fuck 'em than fight 'em,' Ox-Jo whispered wearily.

'You and fucking,' Jap whispered back contemptuously. 'You didn't do her much good back in Cherkassy, did yer? She must have liked that salami sausage of yourn a lot – I *don't* think!'

Colonel Stuermer shifted his position for the umpteenth time, straining at the rope and feeling it cut cruelly into his neck as he tried to get comfortable and at the same time fight off the creeping icy cold. But no matter how he twisted and turned, he was still chilled to the bone. The little woman must know her rope and knots, he told himself wearily.

'What do you think they're gonna do to us, the slits I mean, sir?' Meier hissed, noting Stuermer's movement.

Stuermer shrugged and wished a moment later he hadn't.

'Kill us?' Meier persisted. 'They can't do that. They're slits after all, even if they are Ivans.'

'They say that the female of the species is the more deadly,' Stuermer commented drily.

'Stop that talk!' Roswitha said and jerked her pistol up threateningly.

'We'll take the little slit,' Meier hissed swiftly, and closing his eyes he pretended to sleep.

Now it was two hours later. The other woman was on guard, a shapeless blur in the white gloom of the hut – the primus had long since gone out. But the three men feigning sleep knew that she held a pistol pointed towards them and they knew too that the light was good enough for her to blast them to eternity at any sign that they were attempting to escape.

Still Meier worked on doggedly at his task. Half an hour before, Jap had managed to pass him his bridge and now the big Bavarian was attempting to saw through Colonel Stuermer's bonds with the blunt metal loop that connected the false teeth. It was an immensely laborious business and in spite of the freezing cold, Ox-Jo was sweating with effort. All the same he kept at it, urged on by the knowledge that the blonde woman who had once slept with him would shoot him in the morning as easily as she had once opened her wonderful long legs to let him enter her.

Time and time again, Stuermer bit back a cry of pain, as the rope dug deep into his swollen, chaffed wrists or jerked alarmingly at his throat, as Ox-Jo tugged a little too hard. But he knew, too, that time was running out. He didn't know exactly what he was going to do with the women, if and when Ox-Jo managed to free him; but he told himself he would worry about that eventuality once he was released.

Time passed leadenly. Stuermer cocked his ear to one side to check whether the barely glimpsed figure of the woman in the sleeping bag had nodded off. But her breath seemed the same as ever and he guessed she was still awake, unlike her companion who slept the heavy sleep of the utterly exhausted.

Abruptly he felt a soft crack. Behind him Meier hissed, 'through a bit, sir. Do you think you could use your strength to part more, please?' He heard Meier suck his bleeding fingers.

'I'll try,' he answered through gritted teeth.

With bowed head and hunched shoulders, he made a titanic effort to break the rope, the veins standing out at his temples. The rope gouged deep into his flesh and he bit his bottom lip till the blood came in order to stifle his cry of pain. The damned rope wouldn't give, and in the end, he was forced to say, 'Try a bit more, Ox, I can't do it.'

Meier said nothing, but Stuermer could guess what he was thinking. It would soon be dawn and then it would be too late. The NCO started to saw at the rope with the blunt curved metal once more.

The minutes ground on. Stuermer felt another a soft snap, as yet another strand gave. This time it was the colonel who took the initiative. 'Hang on, Ox,' he hissed, 'I'll have another go.' He took a deep breath, shoulders hunched, the air tight in his lungs. He exhaled and in that same instant raised his shoulders and with all his strength thrust his wrists outwards.

Something gave! He felt the pressure on his swollen wrists relax and it was only with an effort of will that he prevented himself from crying out loud in triumph. He had done it! But in that same moment, the dark figure in the sleeping-bag rose, and behind him Meier gasped with shock, as if he feared that they had been discovered after all.

But they were still in luck. The blonde woman whispered something in Russian to the other woman and struggling into her parka, she crawled through the tunnel outside. 'Going to take a leak perhaps?' Jap suggested in a whisper.

'Perhaps,' Stuermer agreed, knowing that it was now or never. With the other woman outside they stood a much better chance and besides, he guessed that she would not go back to sleep again. Now it was almost dawn and she would want to deal with them and get the dirty business over with. He strained once more and felt his bonds flop to the ground behind him. His wrists were free!

For one brief instant, he massaged his hands to restore the circulation before whispering urgently. 'Quick, Ox, back to me!' Meier reacted immediately.

With fingers that felt like clumsy, thick sausages, Stuermer fumbled frantically with the other man's bonds, ignoring the burning stabs of pain as his nail-less fingers snagged and caught on the knots, scattering fresh gobs of blood on the ground.

'Good enough, sir,' Ox-Jo hissed. 'I can do the rest alone. Take care of the slit.' He grunted and gave a stiffled sigh of relief, which told Stuermer he had freed himself too.

'I'll count up to three, Ox,' Stuermer whispered, 'then I'll go for her. Get ready to tackle the other, if she comes in. No killing if possible ... One ... two ... three. *Now!*'

Stuermer hurtled himself forward from the sitting position. His shoulder socketed into the surprised girl's stomach. The thwack of hard muscle hitting soft flesh filled the hut. The girl's breath came out of her surprised lungs with a sound like a deflating balloon. She sank to the ground while Stuermer sprawled full length. But she did *not* relinquish her hold on the pistol. Much more speedily than Stuermer she sprang to her feet, all breath gone out of her skinny body, but with the pistol raised, finger crooked round the trigger, about to fire.

Meier didn't hesitate one second. He dived forward and collided with the girl. The explosion crashed back and forth in the tight hut, as the two of them – girl and NCO – clung together in its middle, seemingly frozen thus for eternity, both their eyes wide and startled with shock.

Stuermer gazed up at them in awed alarm. For a moment all movement ceased, as if it had been cut off by the blade of a sharp knife. There was nothing but the loud, echoing silence which seemed louder than the clamour which had just preceded it.

Meier, the pistol wrestled out of the girl's limp, dying hand, fired again. In that place the noise was deafening and at that range, the dying girl was lifted clean off her feet. She slammed against the wooden wall, her entrails bulging out above her leather belt, arms extended against the planks, as if she had been crucified there. For one incredible instant she remained thus. Then the life drained from her completely. Eyes wide and empty with death, she slowly crumpled to the floor in the same moment that the alarmed voice from outside cried, '*Lydia*!' and then, obviously in control of her emotions again, harshly and menacingly, '*Stoi, nia dvigatissya*!'

Stuermer did not need to know Russian to understand the threat in those words. 'Quick, Ox, you've got the pistol – through the planks and round the back. I'll draw her fire in the tunnel. You get her from behind.'

'But, Colonel—'

'No buts about it,' Stuermer rapped, knowing just how completely trapped they would be in the hut once they had lost the initiative, 'get a move on!'

Meier waited no longer. Springing over the still tied Jap, who looked up at him reproachfully, he rammed his right boot against the plank to the back of the hut. It snapped and broke at once. Reaching down, he ripped it out with his big paws, as if it were made of matchwood. A second one followed, to reveal packed hard snow. A moment later Meier was burrowing into it like some enormous snow rat.

Stuermer waited to see no more. Gripping the dead girl, his face wrinkled up in self-disgust at what he must do, he started to push her in front of him down the dark tunnel which led to the outside.

'*Stoi*?' the woman outside commanded, her voice a little unsure.

Stuermer sighed his approval. Perhaps the other woman thought the sentry was still alive. He continued his progress towards the patch of milky white, which indicated it would soon be dawn.

Just before he reached the exit, he drew a deep breath and thrust the dead girl in front of him.

'*Lydia!*' He caught the gasp of surprise and shock.

In the same moment that he pushed her outside to fall limp and lifeless into the scuffed snow, the woman screamed, 'You perverted Fritz swine!' and fired a wild volley at the exit.

Stuermer ducked hurriedly. The wood splinters crackled and hissed around his head, as he tried to count the number of slugs she had fired. If she finished the whole magazine, he'd tackle her. If she didn't, and kept him pinned down at the exit, then it would be up to Meier.

Zop! Stuermer ducked low in reflex instinct as another slug hit the planking above his head and splintered it. That was her eighth bullet, he told himself. She must have a nine-slug magazine in her pistol, just as was the case with most German automatics. One more and he'd go for her.

He tensed. There it came. The swift dry crack of a pistol. Another slug hit the wood and splintered it viciously. Stuermer lowered his head and flung himself out across the dead girl's body and into the open.

The blonde cried something he didn't understand. She raised the pistol and took deliberate aim. Stuermer froze in his tracks. He had miscalculated. *Fatally!* The woman was holding a pistol that was unbalanced by an overlong, ungainly magazine. *It was the old-fashioned kind that held twelve bullets!* Stuermer tensed and awaited that slug which would rip open his defenceless flesh and end it all. But Colonel Stuermer was not fated to die – just then.

Just as his horrified eyes made out the sickly white colouring of the knuckle of her forefinger curled round the trigger, which meant she was going to fire the next instant, a dark figure hurtled from round the back of the hut. It was Meier. He had done it! Meier's pistol cracked. In his urgency he missed. The slug kicked up a flurry of angry white snow a metre away from her feet. But the bullet sufficed. Her own pistol shots hissed purposelessly over Stuermer's shoulder.

Fighting for breath, her face suddenly flushed in alarm, the Russian woman ripped off the empty magazine and dropped it in the snow. Walking backwards, not seeming to notice Meier's bullets hissing through the air all around her, she fumbled feverishly for the spare mag. in the pocket of her heavy parka.

As Meier flung down his empty pistol with an angry curse, and prepared to make a headlong rush at the woman before she had fitted the new magazine, Stuermer saw her danger. He didn't want her killed, whatever she might have done to him; she was a woman after all. He opened his mouth and cried frantically, '*Watch out . . . watch out, the drop behind you!*'

The woman did not hear. All her attention was concentrated on fitting the fresh magazine.

'*For God's sake!*' Stuermer roared, his face stricken, ivory-knuckled hands clenched in desperate futility, 'you must watch what—'

The words died purposelessly on his lips. The woman had just rammed home the magazine. He could hear its click quite distinctly above the sound of the wind. Her eyes flashed upwards in triumph as she raised her pistol to kill the two men frozen there into powerless immobility. Her lips opened to say something, which ended in a scream as the ground gave way beneath her feet and the pistol went off purposely into the dirty-white sky and she was suddenly falling into nothing.

Both Stuermer and Meier darted forward. They peered over the edge of the ledge. She was slithering faster and faster, the slither becoming a glissading crazy roll, ever swifter, her scream of fear trailing behind her, getting further and further away until abruptly the snow fell away altogether and she was riding out far, far into the valley, cascading wild blue-white snow behind her. Then Comrade Captain Roswitha Mikhailovna, the founder of the Red Ravens, was gone for ever, and there was nothing left but a loud, echoing silence, which seemed to go on for ever . . .

FIVE

Now the clouds had parted, and the cold sun cast its pink light across the slope ahead. It glittered like a myriad rubies. Above, the twin peaks of Mount Elbrus looked down upon the three tiny figures, in remote mysterious silence.

Colonel Stuermer adjusted the rope looped across his right shoulder more comfortably and drew a deep breath. He let it out in a sudden cloud of grey and commanded, 'All right, let's get on with it!'

'With you, sir!' Meier answered.

'With you, sir!' Jap echoed.

In silence they moved off. The final assault on Mount Elbrus had commenced.

They had been marching upwards for three hours now. The sun had disappeared and the day was grey, with a threat of more snow in the leaden sky. Not that the three men looked upwards much. Their whole attention was concentrated on the rock. Under normal circumstances the fifty-five degree angle of the slope wouldn't have worried experienced mountaineers such as they, but under the thin film of snow which covered the slope, everything was pure ice, so that in spite of constant use of their ice-axes, they slipped time and time again.

But the ice was not their only problem. The altitude was beginning to have its effect again. All of them had splitting headaches, nausea and accelerated breathing. Once, during a five minute break, Colonel Stuermer had checked his pulse and found that it was racing at an alarming rate. He knew what that and the other symptoms meant – they were suffering from altitude fever again. Still they pressed on, climbing steadily along the long humpback ridge which ran southwards from the mountain's eastern peak, down its further side northwest-wards in the direction of the western peak, working now by compass and altitude metre, since the twin peaks had long vanished into the grey gloom.

At eleven o'clock, Stuermer halted and wiped his face before checking his compass and altitude metre, while the other two just stood, panting like two ancient, broken-down cart-horses. 'Five thousand, two hundred metres,' he announced after a minute. 'We've got the worse part behind us.' He paused and waited for some reaction from the two NCOs. None came, so

he said, 'We've got a mere three hundred metres to cover because we're in the dip between the two peaks.'

'A mere three hundred metres, the colonel says,' Meier
gasped with an attempt at his old humour. 'It might as well be
three hundred kilometres for this old Bavarian barnshitter!
Mrs Meier's little boy is *kaputt*.'

Jap did not even smile.

'All right,' Stuermer said, 'The last three hundred metres –
straight up. *March!*'

Linked together by their ropes, digging their ice-axes into
the almost sheer sides of the peak, they worked their way upwards in a zig-zag course with infinite slowness, clinging to
the white surface like tiny human flies.

In the lead, Colonel Stuermer thought he had never been so
cold in all his climbing career. The howling wind, which made
all conversation impossible save by shouts, slashed like steel
knives at their naked bodies beneath the thin clothes, smashed
icy fists into their faces, and ripped the skin off their hands and
lips. In between the gusts, the light glared and waved against
his frozen goggles making it possible to see only through
screwed-up eyes; and all the time the white sludge collected at
his boots and turned them into crippling hobbles.

Now Stuermer and the two other men had forgotten the
peak somewhere above them in the flying white gloom. They
were fighting death, not the mountain; and they had to keep
moving to stay alive. There was no place to move to, save up
or down, and for some reason that their numbed brains could
no longer fathom, they kept moving upwards.

Now it was midday. Still there was no sight of the summit.
Wearily Stuermer wondered if he had made a miscalculation.
He stopped and checked his compass and altitude meter, while
the other two, their shoulders bent, their breath coming like
that of broken-lunged asthmatics, stared numbly at his back.

'Another hundred and twenty metres,' he shrieked above the
howl of the wind. 'Hundred and twenty . . . perhaps another
two hours!' he lied.

The two NCOs said nothing. They waited like dumb animals about to be led into the slaughter house.

'*Aufs geht!*' [1] Stuermer commanded, and they stumbled forward once more.

Now they were working their way upwards with their ice-axes. Step by step, they hewed out their path to the summit. Their faces were crimson with the effort. Even Ox-Jo's massive frame could not stand the strain. More than once he let his ice-axe fall from his great paw and it was only by sheer willpower that he could force himself to bend and pick it up again. The vastness of the mountain became an infinity of rock, ice, snow, seen at the closest range, so that one minute piece of ice resolved itself into a mountain, which had to be assessed, considered, conquered. Stuermer knew they were moving. But when he looked back it seemed that the two bowed figures behind him moved at the pace of tortoises. And all the time the wind howled and shrieked about them, whipping up the frozen snow particles so that they writhed and coiled around their slow-moving feet like white ghosts. Step by step.

Midday. They had been climbing for four and a half hours. Stuermer knew they must have a break. He held up his hand and in their exhaustion the two men behind him almost stumbled into him before they realized he had stopped. 'Break,' he said through lips which were a mass of bloody, black cracks, 'break.'

There was no response from them.

Stuermer dug his hands under his armpits for a moment to warm them a little, while they stood there, swaying on their feet, their eyes behind the goggles blank of any emotion. Stuermer felt that he had insufficient life in his fingers to reach into his pocket. Guiding his right hand into it, taking what seemed an age to open the flap, he pulled out the chocolate bar, which he had saved for this last stage. Not only did it contain dextrose-sugar, but there was also a certain amount of the stimulant pervitin in it. It went against his mountaineer's code of

[1] A mountaineer's command, roughly: 'Up we go!'

conduct to give them it, but without it, he knew, they would never reach the top.

Carefully he broke off a piece of the dark-brown chocolate and shrieked at Meier, 'Open your mouth!'

Numbly, like a very small and stupid child, the big sergeant-major did as he was ordered.

With thick unfeeling fingers, Stuermer slipped the piece between Meier's terribly cracked and swollen lips. There was no reaction. The dark brown square lay on the red wet tongue unswallowed. Stuermer took the NCOs lips and pressed them together. 'Swallow!' he ordered.

Meier swallowed.

With infinite weariness, Stuermer repeated the performance with Jap, before he swallowed a piece himself.

'Now,' he bellowed, feeling the fresh energy already beginning to stream into his unutterably weary limbs, 'fifty metres more and we've done it!'

They reached the western peak of Mount Elbrus in a completely undramatic way, by plodding up the incline, their legs lent new energy by the chocolate, until there was no more incline to climb.

Abruptly before them was a stretch of wind-flattened snow leading to a gentle cone in the centre with, beyond, the sky that – just as abruptly – was beginning to clear to reveal the vast plain below.

Stuermer sat down suddenly in the snow, 'We've reached the summit,' he announced, not having to bellow for the first time in hours, for now the wind was beginning to drop too, as if Nature itself was acknowledging that it had been defeated by these puny mortals.

'This is it, sir?' Meier said incredulously, looking down at the C.O. 'You mean this is all there is to it?'

Stuermer nodded numbly, while the other two stared around in disbelief.

'Well, I'll piss in my boot,' Jap said, 'all that shitty carry-on for this! Was it worth it?'

Stuermer stared up at the outraged look on his wrinkled

yellow face and could feel with him. Was it worth it, so that the ego of some brown-uniformed dreamer could be flattered? He stumbled to his feet and indicated the panorama. 'Out there, Jap, we have Asia – the Caspian Sea, Persia, Afghanistan, India, where our Japanese allies are already fighting. Here, we are as far from Munich as we are from the Persian border. Isn't that something?'

'Give me Munich, a litre of *Löwenbrau,* and a big fat peasant girl with plenty of wood in front of her door, any day,' Meier said, and spat drily in the snow. 'You can—' He stopped suddenly, his eyes keen and alert.

'What is it, you big rogue?' Stuermer asked.

'Out there in the plain. Like a long black snake moving, sir.'

Stuermer focussed his binoculars painfully. At that distance, it was impossible to make out the details of the long column of vehicles; but he knew they had to be military. The average Russian peasant moved by panje-cart [1] and besides, peasants wouldn't move in such huge numbers.

Now he knew why the woman had attempted so desperately to stop them; the Ivans thought Stormtroop Edelweiss was the recce party for a large force to come after them. Now the Soviet High Command was obviously splitting their army so that they could cover both exits from the mountains. That would be a very valuable piece of information for the gentlemen of the staff with their monocles and purple-striped, immaculate breeches.

He dropped his binoculars into their case and turned to the others. 'All right, you two,' he snapped, very businesslike now. 'Who wants to get his ugly mug into the papers – come on, which one of you am I to photograph?'

Ox-Jo looked at Jap, who was already positioning the bravely fluttering Edelweiss flag of the Stormtroop in a cairn of stones, and then back at Stuermer. 'I might not be the answer to a maiden's prayer, sir . . .' he began.

'Yer,' Jap sneered, 'that you can say again – twice!'

'Up yours!'

[1] A pony-drawn vehicle.

'Can't,' Jap retorted, equal to the insult. 'Got a 75 milli-metre field howitzer up there already.'

'Well, as I was saying, sir, before that little owlshit inter-rupted me, I think I'd be more suited. I mean, what would the Führer say if he saw that half-breed's ugly yellow mug star-ing back at him from the front page?'

'Three farts for the Führer!' Jap snarled.

Ox-Jo ignored the remark. 'It stands to reason, sir, that the Führer would prefer to see my own homely-handsome, per-fectly Nordic face looking at him, with all due respect, as be-fits a senior NCO of the High Alpine Corps.'

'Oh, my aching arse!' Jap groaned and clapped his hands to his head in mock anguish. 'Look at the Prussian prick – Nordic! Ow, slap my cheek!'

Stuermer grinned and raised his camera, taking care to en-sure that the lense remained covered until the last moment so that it didn't freeze over. 'All right, build a monkey in front of the flag, Ox-Jo. Here you go, heading straight for history.'

Dutifully Ox-Jo 'built his monkey,' throwing out his mag-nificent chest, his hand clasped rigidly to his cap, staring woodenly, hard-jawed, at the fluttering red-and-white flag.

'Now!' Stuermer snapped and in that instant, he raised his fingers from the lense and clicked the catch down. 'All right, let your guts slip down again. I've got you.'

While Jap and Ox-Jo scraped at the frozen earth around the stone cairn so that they could bury the bottle which contained the scrap of paper on which their three names and the date, '21st August, 1942' were recorded, Stuermer stared out into the far distance.

Somehow he knew, this August day, that he would never see that panorama again. With the clarity of a vision, he knew that this would be the furthest point of the German advance into the Caucasus. The *Wehrmacht* would defeat those un-known Russians down there in the plain time and time again. But in the end the woman (Roswitha had been her name, ac-cording to Meier), and the millions of Russian women and men like her, would beat them. The brown tide had reached its high-water mark.

Totally unexhilarated by his conquest of Mount Elbrus, he turned and said: 'All right, let's get on back . . .'

SIX

On that same night, the radio message flashed from headquarters to headquarters. First from Dietl's Corps HQ; then to Army HQ; from there to Army Command; and, finally, in the early hours of the 22nd August, 1942, it reached the Führer HQ itself. Jodl felt it important enough to wake the Leader at ten o'clock, one hour earlier than his normal rising time. Hitler was a little angry at being wakened early, but Jodl's presence convinced him that the signal must be important. Therefore, he smoothed back his dyed black hair and adjusted the gold-rimmed spectacles, in which it was a punishable offence to photograph the Greatest Captain of all Times, and read it. *'Mission accomplished. At exactly fifteen hundred hours on 21 August, 1942, soldiers of the Alpine Corps planted flag on west summit of Mount Elbrus.'*

His sallow, sickly face lit up. In that characteristic gesture of his, he raised his right knee under his nightgown and slapped his hand down hard upon it. *'Grossartig!'* he exploded. *'Grossartig,* Jodl!'

'Jawohl, mein Führer,' the pale-faced Chief-of-Staff agreed dutifully.

'Now indeed the world will know just what we Germans can do,' Hitler cried exuberantly, pacing the bedroom in his ankle-length cotton nightgown, message clutched in his hand as if it were very precious. 'In the midst of war, our brave soldiers have conquered their greatest mountain. That will show them, friend and foe, that nobody and nothing can stop the German soldier.' He paused in mid-stride. 'Bring them back,' he snapped dramatically. 'Bring them back to Berlin!'

'Bring back whom, *mein* Führer?'

'The men who conquered Elbrus, I want to shake each and every one of them by the hand personally. It will be a triumph, a personal triumph for my brave Bavarians and Austrians of Dietl's Alpine Corps.'

'*Jawohl, mein Führer*,' Jodl answered, and went out to prepare the movement order, telling himself that he hoped he would have nothing to do with the Southern German mountain-hoppers and their cousins from Austria. Mountaineers always seemed to smell so dreadfully of serge, sweat and the mule-shit which they invariably seemed to collect on their big boots ...

Thus the survivors left the mountains : first by mule, then by truck, until finally, after a week of infinitely slow progress, they reached the railhead, where the train which would take them to Berlin was already waiting for them in spite of the demands on transport being made by the new summer offensive.

Just before they embarked to the cheers and jeers and cries of envy of the fresh cannon-fodder going up to the front, Colonel Stuermer, his right hand heavily bandaged still, took one last look at Mount Elbrus, nearly a hundred kilometres away. Suddenly it emerged from a far cloud, drifting up against the dark velvet of the early night sky, the starlight glittering coldly on its twin summits, looking as icy and as remote as a whore's heart.

'*Alles einsteigen*!' the red-capped guard yelled, and waved his metal disc.

His whistle shrilled. The train's wheels shuddered. Steam hissed from the locomotive. Across the way, the cannon-fodder jeered ever louder, knowing that men heading for Berlin would be saved, while they were bound to die on the remote steppe.

'*Alles einsteigen ... der Zug fahrt ab!*'

'I shall never see Elbrus again,' Stuermer whispered to himself, as Greul closed the door of their compartment, 'and I don't want to.'

The train began its long journey to Berlin.

ENVOI

It was 'Führer weather'.

The sky over Berlin was a perfect, cloudless blue, the sun a bright yellow ball, its heat eased a little by the faint wind which blew tiny dust-devils around the elegant riding boots of the generals and the fashionable hems of their ladies' dresses where they stood behind the rope which marked the edge of the parade ground.

All Berlin was there, high Party officials in the chocolate brown uniforms, the elegant senior officers of the Greater General Staff, representatives of the leadership of the youth movements – the *Association of German Maidens, Beauty and Belief*, the *Young Folk*, the ambassadors of Germany's allies, Bulgaria, Slovakia, Rumania, Finland, even the Japanese Ambassador, that bespectacled, grinning, yellow 'honorary Aryan', had turned up to welcome the heroes.

In the middle of the square, the battalion of the 9th Berlin Guards Battalion, every man of them a giant, looking immaculate in their pressed, bemedalled tunics, contrasted strongly with the handful of mountain troops, bronzed and tough-looking, yet awkward and out of place in their brand-new, ill-fitting uniforms. In the midst of that great, smart assembly, the 'heroes of Mount Elbrus', as the Ministry of Propaganda had been calling them these last few days, looked distinctly out of place.

But not all of them were awed by their surroundings. Major Greul was thinking, it will be an honour that my grandchildren will recall; they will say, 'once Grandfather touched the Führer's hand – *he actually did!*' Colonel Stuermer, on the other hand, was telling himself, 'What if I threw his damned medal in his face? What would the Greatest Captain of all Times make of that, eh?' Ox-Jo's thoughts were less idealistic. His wicked Bavarian eyes were roaming the front ranks of the youth movements, quickly eliminating the ugly, frumpish 'folk comrades' of the 'Beauty and Belief movement – 'all belief and no beauty', he told himself scornfully – and fastened onto a particularly well-endowed member of the Association of German Maidens. He jabbed Jap in the ribs, 'Get a load of them lungs, ape-turd! By the Great Joker and all his triangles, I'd like to put—'

'Stillgestanden!' the hoarse voice of the Guards Battalion Commander cut into his words.

The Guards snapped to attention, their gleaming black boots raising a cloud of dust as the steel-shod heels smashed to the ground. To their rear, the band crashed into the Deutschlandlied[1] in a flash of silver and gold.

In the same moment that the last note of the anthem had died away, the hoarse voice of the Guards Commander shrieked, 'Present – arms!'

As one eight hundred pairs of arms completed the intricate drill movement, the slaps of the hard hands against the oiled stocks of the rifles coming in well-drilled unison, a thrilled Major Greul was standing rigidly to attention, his right hand glued to his peaked cap, eyes fixed in fanatic fascination on the well-known, well-beloved figure advancing towards Stormtroop Edelweiss. Dwarfed as he was by his elegant, huge, black-uniformed SS adjutants and bodyguard, there was no mistaking him. It was the Führer!

The band broke into the Führer's favourite march, der Badenweiler, as he presented the first medal, the Knight's Cross of the Iron Cross to Stuermer, taking, as was his custom, Stuermer's right hand in both his after the presentation.

Stuermer did not hear the Leader's words. He was remembering the sense of destiny which had once been the mainspring of his life. Now after all its triumphs and tragedies, it appeared he had lived it only to become this man's instrument: to conquer great mountains in order to further the vulgar, brown dream of this little, sallow-faced, pudgy Austrian.

'You will eat with me this evening, my dear colonel,' Stuermer heard the words, as if they were coming from a great distance, 'I have a bold new project for you and your brave

[1] The German national anthem.

168

men,' and the Greatest Captain of all Times was passing down the row to Major Greul.

One by one, they all received the various forms of the simple black and white cross, then the band was playing the *Fredericus Rex* march, the Guards Battalion was goose-stepping past the saluting base in perfect, mechanical unison, raising great clouds of dust, and that elegant assembly was clapping and cheering and crowding around the handful of shabby mountaineers. Colonel Stuermer stood looking down numbly at the medal hanging from its red and white ribbon from his neck, not hearing the congratulations raining in on him from all sides, not feeling the colonels and generals pumping his hand, not seeing the flash of the cameras, of the men from the Ministry of Propaganda. All that enthusiasm, that human determination, that self-sacrifice – and hadn't that Russian woman been possessed of the same qualities that made mountaineers a different breed? – for this. A cheap piece of metal around one's neck. With sudden determination, Colonel Stuermer pulled the bauble from his neck and stuffed it in his pocket. He must get away from this mob and take a drink to wash the unpleasant taste out of his mouth.

Ox-Jo and Jap were in their element.

The General's wife, who had kept calling them 'my dear, brave boys' and had fumbled with Ox-Jo's flies in the lift, had vanished into the elegant throng; but it didn't worry them. Everywhere the upper-class, expensive room tinkled with medals, champagne glasses, chandeliers; even the tall languorous women, who were everywhere in their afternoon gowns, seemed to the awed soldiers to tinkle, as they moved in that slow way of the rich, who know that they can buy even time with money.

'Devil and a tit!' Ox-Jo exclaimed to his companion, who was feasting his eyes on the mass of powdered bosoms all around him, roughly at the level of his snub nose. 'All you need is the band of the *SS Leibstandarte* [1] and yer'd feel they wanted yer to come, Jap!'

[1] The premier SS division, 'the Adolf Hitler Bodyguard'.

'I'm *coming* already!' Jap whispered in awe, 'I've had ten pairs of knockers pushed in my mug already. I'll swear one of those slits just put her nipple in my mouth a minute ago.'

'Shouldn't walk around with yer snout open,' Ox-Jo commented. 'Yer can catch cold that way. Come on, let's get our paws on all that lovely grub – and I *don't* mean the smoked salmon sandwiches.'

But the two NCOs didn't get far. A tall emaciated woman with dark circles under her eyes, who had once been very beautiful and who was wearing what appeared to be a negligée trimmed with ostrich feathers, put a restraining hand on Ox-Jo's sleeve and giggled, 'The mountain-boys have come down from the hills then.' She giggled again. 'You want champers, or do you backwoods men prefer beer?' She indicated the tableful of drinks behind her. 'Always the best place to be at these affairs.'

'Champagne!' the two NCOs said in unison.

The woman handed them a bottle each and shrieked with laughter when they popped the corks and sent a stream of foaming wine high into the air. 'How symbolic!' she cried to someone else in the thick, sweating throng, that smelled of power and expensive perfume. 'I bet that's the way it is with you mountain boys. Go on, don't bother about glasses, Take it straight from the bottle. *Prost!*

'*Prost!*'

Delicately, his little finger curled, as if he were drinking tea from a fragile piece of porcelain, Ox-Jo took a tiny sip of the bubbling wine and said out of the side of his mouth, 'Make dust, owlshit, she's mine.'

'Make dust yersen,' Jap snarled back, and beamed at the girl. 'She's just my collar size! How good of you to offer us a drink and your excellent company, my dear countess,' he said without a trace of his normal thick Munich accent.

Ox-Jo's mouth fell open stupidly.

'*Not* countess, just a common-or-garden baroness,' the woman replied, and filled her beer-mug with a mixture of champagne and cognac that would have felled an army mule. She downed half of it in one go.

'For me, you are one of nature's aristocrat's,' Jap replied, sipping delicately at his champagne.

The baroness did not seem to hear. 'I hate summer, you know,' she said, apropos of nothing. 'It plays hell with your hair, and the damned sun makes one feel so guilty about staying in bed most of the day.' She downed the rest of the potent mixture and didn't even blink an eyelid. 'You don't think it is a sin to stay in bed, do you?' She looked at them under fluttering lashes in mock innocence.

'Oh, no,' Ox-Jo cried excitedly, finding his tongue at last. 'Bed's always a good place to be.'

'They say he who sleeps does not sin, my dear baroness,' Jap said with his new-found gallantry, his wicked dark eyes darting a fast glance down the drunken woman's startlingly low-cut gown.

'Ah, but my dear little mountain-boy,' she touched his wrinkled cheek in drunken affection, 'I *do* love sin. It is the only thing which keeps one sane in this crazy world.' Her eyes swept the brilliant assembly of Party members and military. 'Don't you think?'

Jap was besides himself with excitement; nobody needed to send him a telegram to tell he was being given an open invitation. 'Of course, my dear baroness, if we are talking about *it* in a medical sense, I am forced to agree.' He grasped her pale hand, tipped with red nails, as if it were dripping blood. 'Would you like, gracious lady, to . . . to . . . sin with a poor common soldier?' He gulped.

'I have been waiting all this long dreary hot afternoon for someone to ask me that question. Come, my little mountaineer,' she offered him her arm graciously. 'I shall show you some peaks that you have never seen before.'

And thus they swept out, leaving an astonished Meier staring after them open-mouthed, wondering just how the little half-breed had pulled it off.

So the men of Stormtroop Edelweiss spent their day in the capital, not seeing the cracks in the facade of the National Socialist 1,000 Year Reich – the yellow, half-starved faces of the shabby workers, the bitter, limbless ex-soldiers everywhere on their crutches, the bombed buildings and piles of brick rubble, the amateur prostitutes in widow's black at every street corner – not wanting to see the misery and the inevitable defeat; savouring greedily their time out of war in the drunken, whoring fashion of soldiers all over the world, knowing as they did so that the call to duty and violent, lethal action must come again soon enough.

Just how soon that would be, Colonel Stuermer, still sober in spite of his decision earlier in the day to get drunk, learned that night.

He had been unimpressed by the cheap neo-classic splendour of the new Reich Chancellory, where the dinner in their honour had been held; he had been unimpressed by the forced frugality of the evening – 'We consume the same rations as the man at the front,' the general, who was his table neighbour had whispered self-importantly, washing down his length of blood-sausage with a vintage burgundy; he had been unimpressed by the high-level talk on cosmic strategy, full of great armoured sweeps into the four corners of the earth, as if these were still the greatest days of May 1940 and not the autumn of 1942; and he had been unimpressed by the cheap, tawdry political designs of the 'golden pheasants' [1] which they hoped to build on victories that had still to be won.

But Colonel Stuermer *was* impressed by the plan that Adolf Hitler began to unfold to him and Greul in the sudden solitude of his study, once the guests had departed, full of drunken bonhomie, to return to their homes to eat a proper meal.

At first Hitler had indulged himself in one of his typical rambling monologues, which eventually turned to the recent murder of SS-*Obergruppenführer* Reinhard Heydrich[2]. 'Men of his kind must know that murderers are always about, with one idea only in their heads – *assassination*!' Hitler said. 'Although that crook Churchill is drunk most of the day, when he is sober he will stop at nothing. Human life means *that* much

[1] High party officials.
[2] Murdered by Czech paras from England in Prague in May, 1942.

to him.' He clicked his fingers together sharply and Stuermer glanced swiftly at an entranced Greul, as if asking him what the devil the Führer was leading up to. 'But two can play that particular game. In '39, the British Secret Service attempted to assassinate me; now they have succeeded with Heydrich. My patience is exhausted. It is their turn now.' He paused, wiped the flecks of foam from the corners of his mouth and looked curiously at the two officers. '*Meine Herren*,' he said, his voice suddenly very low, 'the *Abwehr* [1] has information that all three of them, that bloody murderer Stalin, the drunkard Churchill and the arch-Jew Roosevelt, are to meet together in the coming months, probably in the Persian capital Teheran.' Adolf Hitler paused to let his words sink in. 'Now, a handful of determined men *could* cover the thousands of kilometres over mountain and plain that separate the Persian capital from our lines in Russia and be waiting for these devils in human form, who are out to destroy our beloved Homeland, and then—'

'Then, my Führer?' Major Greul breathed, his eyes glittering fanatically.

'Then there will be a reckoning, a great reckoning . . .'

[1] German Intelligence.

IF YOU HAVE ENJOYED READING THIS ADVENTURE OF STORMTROOP EDELWEISS, WHY NOT READ THEIR NEXT GREAT ADVENTURE, DUE OUT SOON, THE FABULOUS '*OPERATION LONG KNIFE*'?

oxo T